Bad Boys With Expensive Toys

"*Mais, non!*" she replied. "*Mimi* must live with you. It is as your aunt wished."

Esme sent Vince her very white, very perfect I-want-something smile. "Look, if you don't want a dog, I'm sure we could work something out."

He was thinking along the same lines, but then she turned and in the most nauseating indulgent-parent-to-spoiled-little-kid tone said, "Mimi knows her auntie Esme, don't you, sweetums?"

She squatted in front of Mimi's chair, and Vince watched as the dog looked down its nose at her. Then Esme put out her hand, and the dog made a threatening growl, then snapped.

"She's just confused, that's all," Esme said, rising, a mortified blush darkening her cheeks.

"Mimi doesn't like you. Never did," the Frenchwoman said.

"Well, that is simply ridiculous. I suppose you're going to tell me that my cousin here dotes on the dog?"

"No. But the dog dotes on him. *N'est-ce pas,* Mimi? *Tu aimes le grand monsieur, hein?*"

As though cued, the dog jumped off its chair and minced across the floor to leap onto Vince's lap. She circled a few times, as though looking for the most comfortable spot, then sank daintily into a sitting position, making Vince feel like an elephant transporting a tiny, overbred princess. She smelled like Joy perfume, a fragrance he'd forever associate with his aunt.

"Well," said Esme. "I'm sure I don't know why Mimi should be so taken with Vincent. She obviously doesn't know his nickname is Bulldog."

"Hey, it's a mystery to me, too," Vince assured her, not needing Jonathon's smirk to tell him how ridiculous he must look—a muscular guy of six-four with a French poodle nestled in his lap.

"If I might continue?" asked the lawyer.

He read the rest of the will, and it occurred to Vince that neither his aunt nor her lawyer could be called crazy. They'd left nice bequests to the servants, a million bucks each to Esme and Jonathon, and his aunt had given a reasonable sum to charity. Apart from the fact that the main beneficiary was a canine, it was a perfectly sensible will.

Except for the fact that she'd chosen Vince as the mutt's new owner. If Vince ever thought about having a dog—which he did from time to time—he pictured a German Shepherd, big like its owner, the kind of animal that loves to run and isn't afraid of hard work.

A French toy poodle was not on his list.

When Jonathon and Esme had whispered for a few minutes in the corner, Jonathon asked the lawyer, "Once all the bequests are paid out, how much goes to the pooch?"

"After the taxes and duties are paid and all the bequests and claims on the estate settled, Mimi will inherit approximately fourteen million dollars."

While Vince digested that, the heiress snoozed gently in his lap.

"Now, Monsieur Grange," the housekeeper said, "when will it be convenient to move your things into the house?"

"Oh, no." Vince said, gazing around the stuffy library. "I'm staying in my own apartment until this thing's sorted out. I want Mimi to stay here in the house with the staff she's used to. With you," he said in his tough, this-point-is-not-negotiable voice.

"*Pah, non.* This is not possible. André—he was your great-aunt's chauffeur, you know—and I are going back to France to retire." She rose and smiled at him. "All the servants are retiring. I will have Mimi's limousine prepared to transport the two of you home," she said.

"I drove myself here. I'll drive myself home."

She opened her mouth to argue, checked out his expression, and shrugged in that indefinably Gallic way that says, *Be an idiot, see if I care.*

"Very well. I will have her things delivered to you."

Oh, right. There'd be a dog dish, probably some priceless antique, and the leash. If it matched the collar, he and the dog were going to be mugged every time they went outside the door.

The Frenchwoman patted the dog on the head. *"Soyez gentille,* Mimi. *Je t'aime,"* and she kissed the blue-rinsed topknot and straightened, sniffing with emotion.

"Oh, and remember," she said to Vince, "Mimi only speaks French."

Two

"*Viens-ici,* you little rug rat," Vince bellowed, deciding that after the twenty-four hours he'd had, the little powder puff on legs better not push him.

If she didn't come back in thirty seconds, he was going to get one of Uncle David's hunting rifles, put a bullet through the Parisian pooch, and have her stuffed to hang on his wall like a trophy.

"I know you understand English, you little varmint." Ahead of him he saw the bouncing curls of Mimi's ears as the dog carefully squatted and squeezed out her two hundredth drop of pee. He didn't have time for this. He didn't want to be seen with this embarrassment of a dog. If the media caught wind of his new accessory, his career as a tough labor negotiator was over. Bulldog? Hah, they'd be calling him Pierre.

Since the dog was keeping up the pretense that it didn't understand a word he was saying, he grabbed the French/English dictionary he'd bought last night in desperation.

"*Viens-ici,*" he shouted. Then he flipped a few pages. "*Ou je* going to, going to, *je va* wring your hairy little neck."

Somewhere close by, he heard a woman's soft laughter. Oh, shit. He'd taken today off, waiting until everyone was at work, and bypassed the park nearest his place in Hell's Kitchen for the anonymous expanse of Central Park so he'd be as good as invisible.

He glanced up and promptly dropped his book on the ground. In front of him was the most beautiful woman in the world. Dark sultry eyes, rich black hair, lips so plump and red he couldn't help but fantasize about cherries, and a body to make a man weep with frustrated desire. She wore black pants and a black-and-white sweater that clung in a lot of very interesting places.

"It's *viens-ici,*" she said, in a voice that reminded him of Audrey Hepburn. "You don't pronounce the 's,' and it's *"je vais,* not *je va,"* she bent down to pick up his dictionary which she handed back to him with a smile.

"You speak French," he said in a daze.

She laughed again, and he thought that sound ought to be age restricted. "I am French."

"Would you do me a big favor and call my dog? She only understands French. Or so she pretends."

The woman didn't seem to find a French dog in the middle of New York at all strange. "Of course, what is its name?"

He cringed. "Mimi."

"Mimi." the woman called in a clear, sexy tone. *"Viens-ici, je te donnerai un petit biscuit."*

At the first words, he'd seen the little white fiend perk up its head and turn. As she spoke, its head cocked from side to side as though listening for a trick. Then, suddenly, just when Vince had pretty much decided it was either the shotgun or the pound, there was a flurry of blue-rinsed white, a scatter-shot of yippy-yappy barks, and Mimi was prancing at the woman's feet, her little pink tongue hanging out and a patch of dirt clinging to one of her pristine paws.

"Oh, que tu es mignonne," the woman said, scooping the dog up into her arms, for which Vince, too stupid from lust to realize he should have grabbed the dog when he could, was more than grateful.

"Look, children, a sweet little dog."

Children? Vince turned around in shock to see a child of about nine and one of about five standing there regarding him. He didn't even realize he'd been fantasizing about getting to know this amazing woman better, until it occurred to him with a double shock that she was both wife and mother.

"We're not supposed to talk to strangers, Mademoiselle Veneau," said the oldest—a humorless-looking girl in some kind of uniform with a kilt.

Vince might not know much French, but he knew mademoiselles weren't married. His world began to right itself.

"Vince Grange," he said, bowing slightly to the children and then extending his hand to the French woman.

She took it, and he was immediately struck by how much better she looked with Mimi in her arms than he ever would. "Sophie Veneau," she said, with that gorgeous lilt to her voice that made him want to swap places with Mimi and take over the job of licking her neck.

She passed him back the dog and said, "Come, children. We must go to the pediadentist."

As she walked away, Mimi whined softly. Vince knew how the dog felt.

He wanted to ask Sophie for her phone number at least, but with the elder girl glaring at him as if he were a skanky pervert, he decided against it. He had a name now. In a city of nine million people, how hard could it be to find one Sophie Veneau?

Then little miss stuck-up did him an unexpected favor. "You know, mademoiselle, if my mother hears about this incident, she'll probably report you to the Tyler Agency."

Sophie's response was, *"En français, s'il te plaît,* Morgan."

The pint-size troublemaker scowled and spoke in French, and soon they were beyond his hearing range.

Vince wasn't stupid enough to put the dog down again, and since it had had plenty of exercise running away when he called it, it seemed content to be carried half hidden in his coat like a wino's bottle.

But, in spite of one full day of poodle-induced torment, Vince was smiling broadly. For the first moment since he'd been saddled with Mimi, he wondered if Great-aunt Marjorie might have done him a favor.

In the twenty-four hours since he'd inherited Mimi, Vince had discovered that he needed help. If he was out, the dog howled, his neighbors had informed him. This was bad. Worse, it needed regular trips outside and a gourmet chef to prepare its meals.

He'd scoffed when the limo pulled up in front of his building and delivered Mimi's things, which included a Limoges china set of dishes, for the dog's exclusive use, a book of handwritten recipes of Mimi's favorite foods, and her appointment diary. She had a standing appointment at Bliss for a weekly manicure, she was scheduled for a hair appointment in two weeks, and her doctor made house calls. The doctor was French.

André, who'd delivered Mimi's limousineful of her special things before Vince's bemused gaze, had hauled in a case of Perrier, and that had struck Vince as the final straw.

"You have got to be kidding."

Andre had sniffed. "It is all she drinks, monsieur."

"You mean she doesn't slurp Dom Perignon with every meal?"

"Alcohol is not good for dogs, monsieur."

"Mimi, my friend," Vince had said, as he looked at all the stuff littering his apartment, "things are going to change."

The first change he made was to go out and get a couple of cans of dog food. He didn't want to shock her little system too much, so he dumped the stuff on one of her fussy hand-painted plates with the gold rims. He even poured her Perrier into one of the fruity little china bowls.

She drank a little Perrier, lapping it with her tiny pink tongue, but she didn't so much as acknowledge the existence of the plebian dog food.

Sooner or later, Vince figured, she'd get hungry, and she'd eat.

In twenty-four hours it still hadn't happened, and now the dog food had a brown crusty overlayer. He wasn't a cruel man at heart, and he didn't think he could handle it if the dog starved to death.

He also wasn't going to cook up its special foods. That was plain ridiculous.

And there was the little communication problem he and his new pet were having. He only spoke English. The dog only understood French. Privately, he thought she was putting him on, but she was doing a damn good job of driving him into the nuthouse.

What Mimi needed, he realized in a blinding flash of brilliance, was a French nanny. More to the point, what Vince needed was Sophie Veneau.

The Tyler Agency was amazingly easy to find. Vince made an appointment with the agency's president for later that day—explaining that his case was an emergency.

The woman who owned the agency tried to convince him that they didn't hire out dog nannies; then she tried to convince him that Sophie Veneau was unavailable.

Vince smiled at her. He'd ended vicious strikes, negotiated settlements between teamsters and multinational trucking companies. One little nanny agency was a piece of cake. Every time the woman objected, he simply upped the price he was willing to pay. Or that Mimi was willing to pay. With fourteen mil, an extravagant nanny salary was chicken feed to Mimi.

"Please, Mr. Grange," Ms. Tyler said at last, when she was flustered, torn between her rules and Mimi's money, and he knew he had her, "I can't simply take a nanny away from a family. They have a contract."

"I'm not asking you to, Ms. Tyler," he assured her. "Naturally, I'll pay the wages of their new nanny until the end of the contract."

"Well," she hesitated.

"And, of course, I'll pay an extra bonus to the agency to cover your trouble."

"Ms. Veneau will have to be agreeable."

"Of course," he said. After seeing the obnoxious elder daughter, he suspected Sophie would swap her for a poodle any day. At least until she saw the menu plan. But, by then, he'd have her.

He gave the Tyler woman his phone numbers, a couple of character references, and a hefty deposit.

"Well," she said, "I'm making no promises, but I'll see what I can do."

He wasn't surprised at all when he answered his phone later that evening to hear the sexy tones of Sophie Veneau on the other end. Mimi yipped a couple of times when the phone rang, but soon settled back into his lap, the only place she'd stay put when he was around.

Great. His own personal chastity poodle. Unless he could get her sorted out, his sex life was over. And he wasn't giving that up, not even for fourteen million bucks.

Some things were priceless.

"Am I speaking to Mr. Grange?"

"Yes, but it's Vince."

"Very well. I understand you want me to be the nanny for your dog."

It hadn't occurred to him that he might be insulting this woman by trying to hire her for Mimi, and now he was smitten by conscience. "I hope I didn't . . . I mean, would you be interested at all?"

Her sigh fell soft as a spring breeze on his ear. "Frankly, it would be wonderful to spend the day with a creature who doesn't keep threatening to report me to the Tyler Agency."

Vince laughed, the tightness in his chest easing now he knew he hadn't insulted the woman. "So, when can you start?"

"I understand it is an emergency?"

"Yes. I can't go to work and leave Mimi. She's . . ." He looked down at the ball of fluff too tiny to be so much trouble. "She's a little high-strung."

"Surely you want a dog trainer, Mr. . . . Vince."

"No. I want you."

There was a moment's silence, and he shut his eyes. "That, as you French would say, was a faux pas."

She laughed. "It was, indeed."

"I meant that you speak French and Mimi took to you right away. She doesn't need dog obedience, and she's house trained. It's that she's used to being with people all the time. French people."

"I see. If you don't mind me saying so, she seems an odd choice of dog for you."

"I don't mind you saying so at all. I didn't choose her; she was willed to me." It occurred to him that he probably shouldn't explain that Mimi would probably head the Forbes list of the country's richest canines.

"I see."

"She's a little spoiled. She has to have her food specially prepared. Could you handle that?"

"I think so. I'm a very good cook."

Of course she was; she was French.

"So, will you give it a try?"

"Yes."

"Great. Can you start tomorrow?"

"You must know I can. The family were quite happy to let me leave early since you're going to pay for their next slave until the contract is up."

He chuckled. "That bad, eh?"

"Impossible. Give me your address. And what time tomorrow?"

When he'd done that, he tried to think of something to say that might keep her on the phone a little longer, but she forestalled him.

"I'd better get ready for tomorrow, then. I will see you and Mimi in the morning."

"Good night," he said.

"Tell Mimi *bonne-nuit. À demain.*"

"Mimi, she said good night. And I'm pretty sure she said, I de man."

Three

Sophie had never imagined when she'd trained at the Cordon Bleu in Paris that she'd one day be called upon to prepare Escalopes de Veau Chasseur for a dog.

Of course, she hadn't imagined back in those days that she'd end up in New York as a nanny, either.

Bien sûr, there was a demand for a woman who could teach the little Brittanys and Murphys, the Adams and Zacharys, a second, or third, or fourth language while she walked them to school, drove them to ballet, Karate, and Junior Achievers. In her last job, she was also supposed to cook elegant gourmet meals for the children of the family so they'd grow up with refined palates.

She shuddered to think of the number of meals she'd prepared and then quietly thrown out. If a child wanted to eat like a child instead of a sophisticated diplomat, she tended to look the other way. Still, her work was lucrative, and for the most part, she enjoyed it.

However, she was certain a little dog was going to be no trouble at all in comparison to her usual overachieving charges. And at least she wouldn't have to teach Mimi French as they walked the park every day. *La petite chienne* was French.

It wasn't her language skills but her culinary ones that Mimi was in need of. Bah, the stuff that man had put in her bowl was *dégoutant,* when Mimi was obviously used to the best of cuisine. The dog clearly needed her, and she was happy to help.

No. It wasn't Mimi who put a frown between her brows and a sliver of unease beneath her ribs; it was the dog owner who did that. Monsieur Vince was going to be a problem.

Une grande problème.

A big, tall, brawny problem with eyes that were like slow, sleepy sex. She shivered just a little when she remembered the way he'd looked at her.

Well, she couldn't turn down a fellow Frenchwoman in a time of need, especially when her sparkly leash was attached to a man who couldn't speak her language or give her decent food to eat.

She'd been attracted to him from the first moment she saw him struggling over a French/English dictionary looking huffy and helpless. Though, if he were responsible for the blue rinse in Mimi's hair, she might have to reconsider her attraction to the man. Except there was something so sexy about a big, virile hunk with a tiny poodle in his arms. She got the same melting sensation when she saw a macho young guy with a baby. So sweet, with all that power, cradling such a small creature so he appeared both endearingly clumsy and reassuringly protective.

She'd dressed for her new job with more than usual care, certain that a dog who sported a fresher manicure than Sophie was going to notice.

She struggled into the skin-tight jeans she'd bought in Italy last year, paired them with the sage green cotton designer shirt she'd bought on sale at a little boutique off the Champs Elysée. Her boots were from a Prada sample sale, her sweater from Bloomingdales. She was an international fashion maven.

Since she wasn't about to be outshone in the jewelry department by a canine, she stuck with small gold hoops in her ears and left it at that.

As she sped to her destination on the subway, she knew she hadn't really dressed for Mimi. Mimi, for instance, didn't care that her lingerie (also French, naturally) was absurdly wispy and utterly decadent. Sophie was Gallic enough, and fatalistic enough, to accept that sexual attraction happened. She couldn't help her unmistakable lust for her new employer. She could, however, decide when or if it should be acted on.

In this case, she hadn't yet made up her mind.

Still, her pulse skipped a little when she walked into her new employer's building on Forty-fourth and announced herself to the doorman.

The dog began barking hysterically when Sophie knocked on the door of 17A. The timbre of the barking changed when Vince opened the door and Mimi clattered across the hardwood floor, her manicured nails like two pairs of castanets.

No sooner had she sniffed Sophie than her barking changed from hysterical fear to hysterical excitement, as she leaped in the air a few times, then rose on her hind legs and turned three perfect circles.

Sophie laughed and looked at Vince, who stared at the twirling poodle as if it were a new—and possibly deadly—life form.

Having twirled seven or eight times, her ears flying around her head like fluffy blue-tinged propellers, Mimi abruptly dropped back to all fours, staggering a little as though dizzy and looking expectantly at her audience.

Sophie broke into laughter and clapped her hands. *"Oh, que tu es adorable!"* she cried, at which Mimi, delighted to hear her own language, spun faster. Then she pawed the air until Sophie scooped her up and pressed a kiss to her fluffy head, which appeared to Sophie to have been backcombed.

She held the dog to her breast as she looked up, and up, at Vince towering over her.

He wore almost the same thing he'd worn yesterday. Jeans, a T-shirt that revealed muscular arms and hinted at an equally muscled torso, and casual leather tie-up shoes. His hair, she noted, was still damp from his shower.

"I have to leave for work soon, so we'd better go over the ground rules."

Such a serious owner for such a sweet little dog. "All right."

She tore her gaze away from the man who was as magnetic as he'd been the day before, more so in the confines of an apartment where he seemed bigger, his presence more potent. She stepped all the way inside and took her first good look at the apartment.

Compared to her minute efficiency sublet, this seemed enormous. A big, open room combined living and dining, and she suspected he'd knocked out walls to make one big space. Even the kitchen was open. A couple of large windows offered a view of the Hudson River. The walls were white. For décor he had a calendar from some football team, one very nice, large abstract canvas, and a black-and-white framed photograph of Hell's Kitchen in the twenties.

His furniture was fairly standard American bachelor fare. A big plasma TV dominated the living area, and a comfy chair, obviously Vince's favorite, faced the TV. A few magazines that looked like sports and business sat on the side table, and a second table flanked a gray leather sofa.

The kitchen was spotlessly clean but a little sterile. Something she'd soon change.

"This is Mimi's cookbook," he said, walking her into the galley kitchen and pointing to a binder on the kitchen counter. "She only eats stuff out of there."

"Really?"

"Yep. I got some things, but I put some cash in an envelope inside the front cover if you need—I don't know, spices or something."

"Definitely I will need spices. Don't you have any?" Who could survive without spice?

"Sure I do." He sent her a grin that made her pulse speed. "Salt and pepper." He tilted his head to one side, and his eyes crinkled at the corners in a disturbingly attractive way. "And mustard. Is mustard a spice?"

"Not in my kitchen." She understood now what he'd meant when he said his case was an emergency.

She put Mimi, who was wriggling, down, and the dog pranced down the hallway toward one of two closed doors.

"And this is where I keep a spare key," he said, pulling open a drawer and taking out a key chain with a tiny football on the end, "which you'll need when you go out."

She nodded, noting Mimi had reached the door and was scratching. Still listening, while Vince explained how to get in and out of the apartment, she crossed and opened the door for Mimi.

She blinked. Inside was a double bed with a bright pink satin bedspread and a headboard shaped like a tiara. On it, in silver script, was the word *Princess*. There were rhinestones dotted here and there.

"And this is . . ."

"Mimi's room," Vince said sharply.

"Oh, I'm so relieved," she said, then, realizing how she'd sounded, added hastily, "I mean, it's nice for her to have a place of her own to . . ." She broke off when Vince opened the other door as though he needed to prove a point. His cheeks sported a slight ruddiness that hadn't been there before.

"*This* is my room," he said. One peek told her it was a shrine to testosterone. A big, sturdy-looking bed with a hefty pine headboard and a plain navy cotton spread that gave off the indefinable air of having seen a lot of action. There wasn't much else in the room. A deep armchair with a reading light beside it, a simple chest of drawers with a dish of change on the top. It was, like the kitchen, clean and simple. Nothing fussy or feminine at all. In fact, Vince could have come from central casting as a rough, tough he-man but for the effete Mimi in his life. From where she was standing she could see into both bedrooms, and her sense that these roommates were a very odd couple grew.

"Mimi seems an odd choice of pet for you."

Vince puffed his cheeks and let out a sigh. "I think I'm going to have to explain that to you. Mimi's very . . . precious."

"Yes, she is."

"What I mean is . . . I told you I inherited her from my aunt. She pampered that thing and treated it like a baby. Like the baby of royalty, to be precise. I promised I wouldn't let anything happen to the dog."

"Oh, how kind of you to look after your aunt's cherished pet."

He shifted, visibly uncomfortable with her praise, which only made her think him more adorable.

"I got her a couple of days ago, so we're still getting used to each other. She—uh—sleeps in the other bedroom, in her own pink silk bed." She could have sworn that those rugged, already-stubbly-at-eight-in-the-morning cheeks, deepened slightly more in hue. "Theoretically." He glanced down at Mimi. "She gets lonely, and if I don't let her in with me, she starts barking and whining and scratching on the door."

She suppressed a smile. "I see." And she did see. The mental picture of that big man in his big-man bed with little Mimi curled up beside him did something to her insides. She was going to have to have a stern talk with her hormones; they were acting foolish. She sighed. Again.

Well, her hormones hadn't led her too far astray. All the way from Paris to New York, certainly, but she liked it here. Even though she'd soon lost her liking for the young man she'd crossed the ocean to be with.

"So, you'll need to walk her. And you have to keep her on a leash or she won't come back."

"It's your French," she said, shaking her head. "That's why she won't come when you call. She doesn't understand. We'll have to work on teaching you some French, *oui*, Mimi?"

He appeared stunned at the idea. Speechlessly so.

She smiled at him. "But it's only logical. Your dog speaks French. You will have to learn."

His tough-guy eyes narrowed. They were an attractive mix of green and gray and blue, she'd noted. There was a name for that, which she could never remember.

"Why can't Mimi learn English?"

"She's a dog. How many multilingual dogs do you know?"

"A dog needs a master," he said a mite huffily. "I am Mimi's master."

"Not if she doesn't understand a word you say."

"Here's the leash." He pulled out a length of chain with a clip on one end and a black leather strap on the other that looked as though it had been manufactured for prison guard dogs. "And her collar. I'm having trouble getting her into it. Maybe you can explain in her own damn language that she has to put it on before she can go out."

He handed her a black leather collar appropriate for a very large, very fierce Rottweiler. Or an over-the-top S & M party.

Mimi took one look at the contraption and minced away with her nose in the air.

"But what happened to her beautiful sparkly collar?"

"She can't wear that around here. She'll get mugged."

"Mugged? But they're only crystals . . ."

She stopped when he shook his head. "Cartier. It's a custom job. There are twenty carats of flawless diamonds in that collar."

"Well. Well, she can't wear this."

Seeing he was about to argue, she said, "Never mind. Mimi and I will sort it all out, *n'est pas mignonne?*"

Mimi's pom-pom tail wagged, and her head came up.

Sophie patted Vince's shoulder reassuringly and felt strong muscle that made her want to purr. For a second she envied Mimi being able to curl up beside him in that big bed.

He stared down at her for a long moment, and his shoulder seemed to warm beneath her palm. She felt that insistent and inconvenient quiver of arousal again deep in her belly.

"I have to go," he said suddenly, when the moment had moved beyond comfortable. "I've got a meeting."

"Have a good day." She smiled and took her hand back, resisting the urge to shake the heat from it.

"Thanks. You've got my numbers?"

"Yes. Don't worry."

As soon as Vince was gone, she lapsed into French, thinking Mimi must miss hearing her own language. First, she read through all the recipes, found a veal one that she could easily adapt for Vince's dinner. As he'd warned her, his kitchen was woefully ill-equipped.

She scrawled a list of essentials, helped herself to some cash from the envelope, and then picked up the leather-and-chain monstrosity. She managed to coax her reluctant charge into it, but the weight of the collar bowed Mimi's little fluffy head, and the chain dragged on the ground.

"Bah," she said in frustration. "My poor bébé, it's not for you."

She replaced the original diamond collar on a much happier Mimi. She'd have to hope everyone made the same assumption she had that the stones were rhinestones, because neither she nor Mimi were going to be seen with that black leather and chain.

With Mimi happily prancing beside her with her own diamond-studded collar and leash, they left the apartment.

It was a gorgeous fall day, and she was being paid a great deal of money to spend time with the nicest charge she'd ever had.

Life was sweet.

While they stopped every few steps for Mimi to mark her trail, Sophie wondered what vegetables Vince liked, which was appropriate since she'd cook his dinners for him, and she wondered if any female but Mimi was sharing his bed with him, which was inappropriate, but truthfully occupied her mind a lot more enthusiastically than the man's vegetable preferences.

Which was probably why she didn't pay her usual attention to what was going on around her.

She'd followed Vince's directions to a small local park, which appeared empty. She heard a pounding of feet on the gravel path, which she dimly supposed was an enthusiastic jogger, until she was shoved from behind and a gloved hand grabbed at the sparkling leash. She screamed in a combination of surprise, fear, and shock, instinctively tightening her hold on Mimi's lead as she fell painfully to her knees on the gravel path.

Furious at herself for being taken unawares, she grabbed her purse and swung up and back. She heard the impact of her bag against a solid object, followed by a grunt of pain. Mimi was snarling and yapping, nipping at the black-gloved hand that was pulling at the leash.

She was getting ready to sink her own teeth into the hand that was trying to haul the leash from her so hard she was getting a burn on her palm.

She cursed in French, knowing she and Mimi couldn't hold on much longer, as she used her free hand to dig in her bag for her mace.

She found it, yanked the cap off with her teeth even as she wondered if her wrist would be permanently damaged from the strain of the pulled leash. She squirted a stream of mace over her shoulder and heard a violent curse as suddenly the pressure eased on the leash.

She turned, ready to use her fingernails on the guy's face, when she heard a low, fierce growl. Stunned, she turned to stare at Mimi, but the poodle looked as surprised as she.

She turned her head in time to see a big black shadow launch itself at a tall man in a low-pulled woolen cap who was furiously wiping his streaming eyes.

This time the howl of surprise and pain came from the attacker. She sensed rather than saw the dog bite and shake—looking like a vengeful black demon—his growls as ferocious as his teeth. She pulled Mimi to her, feeling she'd stumbled into a nightmare, and suddenly she was free.

Their attacker was running toward a beat-up looking sports car, a hand covering his face, the other holding his butt.

"Bastard bit me in the ass," he yelled. The big black dog in question raced behind the man, growling and snapping. She saw the passenger door open even as the engine gunned. The miscreant threw himself into the car, but the black dog got one more piece of him, coming away with a patch of denim, the back pocket still attached.

She watched, bemused, as the car tore away. She squinted at the license plate, but it was so grimed with dirt it was unreadable. Deliberately, no doubt.

Now that the car was gone, Mimi was doing her best to imitate the big black dog. Barking and pulling at the leash, growling as ferociously as a toy poodle can.

The black dog, she now saw it was a Doberman, raced back to her side. She flinched involuntarily as the powerful jaws ground at the denim and wrestled it back and forth almost as though he suspected the owner might still be in the pants.

Then, suddenly, he dropped the mashed fabric at her feet, wagged his tail, and let his tongue hang out, a dog well pleased with himself.

"Good dog," she said carefully, still hanging on to her mace, wondering if the ferocious Doberman was ready for some new prey.

But at the words, *good dog,* he wagged his tail harder and gazed at her adoringly.

Suddenly she laughed, almost light-headed with relief. Sophie pulled Mimi up into one arm and put her other around the Doberman's neck. She had the dubious pleasure of having her neck licked by one small dainty tongue, and half her face slobbered on by the size-large, heavy-on-the-saliva version. "Good dogs. Good, good dogs," she said, hugging them closer.

Four

Realizing she couldn't sit on the ground all day cuddling dogs, she rose to her feet and ignored the impulse to bolt back to Vince's apartment and lock herself and Mimi inside.

She'd failed on her first day. Vince had told her not to take Mimi out decked in diamonds, and she'd disobeyed his orders.

But she was Mimi's nanny, and Mimi still needed a new collar, a new leash, and some food. That's what she was going to get, and no park mugger was going to stop her. She picked up the tooth-marked piece of denim and looked in the pocket, but it was empty, leaving no clue to the owner. Still, the patch of cloth itself was a clue of sorts, so she folded it and stuffed it into her bag along with her recapped mace.

She was a lot less carefree as she made her way through the rest of the park, but no violent criminals approached, no one but a few dog walkers like herself and a couple of mothers chattering away, pushing strollers containing infants.

The big dog never left her side, and after suggesting a couple of times that he go home, she gave up and was grateful for his company. He'd proven himself her and Mimi's champion, and she decided, when she was at the butcher, that he deserved a treat.

Mimi pretended—or perhaps felt—no interest in the package from the butcher, but the Doberman drooled and licked his chops as they traced their way back through the park. She came upon the spot where they'd met him, and she handed him the big meaty bone with a pat on the head and her thanks. He took the bone in a surprisingly delicate manner that charmed her and dropped down on his oversized paws to gnaw at it. But as soon as she and Mimi resumed their journey, he picked up his bone and followed.

Sophie bit her lip. What to do? He wore no collar, and no one seemed to be looking for him.

"You have to go home now, Sir Galahad," she said, as firmly as she could. He wagged his tail and kept following her.

Mimi was no help; she could swear the little scamp was flirting with their big, dark protector.

When they reached Vince's apartment, the dog seemed disappointed but not surprised not to be invited in. He settled on a small patch of grass beside the entrance and resumed devouring his bone.

"Hiya, buddy," Vince said when he arrived home from work to find a black Doberman wagging its stub of a tail at him. A bleached-looking bone lay at his feet. "Now this is what a real dog looks like," he said as he rubbed its head, wondering vaguely where the owner was.

Once Vince reached the door to his apartment he hesitated for a second, then knocked before putting his key into the lock on his own door. It seemed appropriate to knock when there was a woman inside—a woman he was neither related to nor sleeping with.

He opened the door and was immediately struck by mouth-watering smells of dinner cooking, by the hysterical yappy delight of Mimi, and by the fact that his nanny had a rip in her jeans, a bandage on her knee, and she seemed to be limping.

Bending to give Mimi an absent pat, he never took his gaze off Sophie. "What happened?"

She glanced at him and away again, and in that instant their gazes connected she looked guilty as hell. "I'm so sorry," she said, stirring something on the stove, which put her back to him. "I did a very stupid thing."

His fourteen million dollar toy poodle was safe, so he figured he could handle her stupidity, but he wasn't happy that she'd ended up limping on her first day working for him. "What happened?" he asked a second time, more mildly.

When she didn't answer right away, he walked up behind her in the small kitchen and touched her shoulder. "This might be easier if we sat down and discussed it face-to-face. Unless Mimi's missing or you're quitting, it can't be that bad."

She smiled absently and sat at the pine table she'd already set for one.

"You didn't have to cook for me," he said, trying not to think about how pathetic the table looked with one place mat, one fork, one knife. She'd even folded a napkin and laid it beside the fork. He usually ate in front of the TV if he was eating at home alone, which he didn't do very often. Pre-Mimi that was. He now realized he was going to have to change his ways or get some extra dog-sitting help.

"Cooking for the family is part of my job. I enjoy it," she said, then drew a deep breath. "I took Mimi out with her expensive collar on today," she said quickly. "She wouldn't wear the other, and I thought I'd take her straight to the pet shop and get her a new one that she liked."

"And?"

"We were mugged."

"What?" The hell with the dog, he couldn't believe some thug had messed with Sophie. "I can't . . . How did it happen? When?" He shoved a hand through his hair. "Where?"

"In the park, the one you gave me directions to. A man knocked me down and grabbed for the leash. I-I should have known better. You told me not to use the good collar and leash. I'm very sorry."

"So he took the diamond dog stuff and left it at that?" Relief was hammering through his veins. New York was a lot safer than it had once been, but there was still too much violence. He hated to think of what could have happened.

"No," she said with a small smile. "He didn't get anything. Mimi was very brave and bit his hand."

At the sound of her name, Mimi danced over to lick Sophie's fingers.

"That gave me a chance to get to the mace in my purse. But we still would have been in trouble without our rescuer."

"Thank God. Who was it? Another dog walker? A cop?"

She shook her head. "Another dog. A big black Doberman. He was so very fierce and bit the mugger and chased him away until the man jumped in a car and sped away."

His relief that his nanny and his dog were safe was such that he didn't care if the would-be thieves had flown away on magic carpets. They were gone, and no one was badly hurt. At least he hoped not.

"How bad's the knee?"

"Not bad. I cleaned it and put some of your antiseptic on it, and a bandage."

"Good."

"So, if you don't trust me anymore with Mimi, I will understand."

"Sophie, I'm going to take you myself to get a new collar and lead. I'm the one who should apologize."

"We already got one." She looked down at Mimi. *"Allez, va montrer ton nouveau collier à ton maître."*

Mimi pranced to the corner, and Sophie followed, pulling out a slim red leather lead and matching collar. "At least there are no rhinestones," he said, trying to look on the bright side.

She laughed softly. "Mimi really preferred the pink. I had to put my foot down."

He laughed back at her, watching her with the lead that appeared so elegant in her hand. Her gaze rose to his, and a sizzle went through him that should have scorched the floor.

She turned and made a production of putting the lead away. "Well, Mimi's fed. Your dinner is ready whenever you are. The salad is in the fridge. I'll see you tomorrow if you're not firing me."

"Stay and eat with me," he said. He didn't want her to leave, not after he'd spent so much of the day thinking of her here, looking forward to seeing her at the end of his workday.

"Oh, but . . ."

"I've got some wine in the fridge. It's crazy for me to eat here alone and you to go home and eat alone . . . that is, if you live alone," he said, mentally crossing his fingers that her answer would be affirmative.

She put her head to one side. "I do."

"Well, then."

"Well, then." But she didn't move.

"I'm thinking of Mimi," he said, grasping at straws, anything to make her stay.

"Mimi?" Those wonderful, plump, cherry-colored lips curved in a smile.

"Yes. While we eat, you can teach me French so I'll be able to communicate with my dog."

"Bien sur."

"I'm hoping that means 'yes.' "

"It means 'very well.' Now you say it." She removed the tea towel she'd worn around her hips like a very sexy chef and walked toward him, so he did his best to repeat the phrase, which made Mimi bark and Sophie laugh.

Oh, well. It was a start.

He retrieved wine from the fridge and a couple of glasses, and she dished up. "Mmm. That smells incredible. What is it?"

"Escalopes de Veau Chasseur." She grinned impishly. "I

made a version for Mimi from her special book. This is the human equivalent."

He glanced up. "You're feeding me dog food?"

It wasn't Audrey Hepburn she reminded him of, he realized. It was Juliette Binoche, the actress he'd seen in *Chocolat*. Sophie had the same mischievous twinkle in her eyes and a sexy way with her in the kitchen . . . although Juliette hadn't fed Johnny Depp any dog food.

"Don't worry, Mimi's menu would rival Maxim's in Paris."

Five

"So, tell me about yourself," he said, once he'd determined that her food tasted as good as it smelled, which he did by cleaning his plate in about two minutes.

"Would you like some more?" she asked in a bemused tone, looking at his naked plate.

"Oh, yeah," he said. "Sorry, there's a lot of me to fill."

She had to admit he was right. Tall and solid, he was a man who begged to be fed. Perfect for a woman who loved to cook.

Once she'd given him another helping, and watched him deliberately try to slow the pace of his eating, he asked again, "You were going to tell me about yourself."

"Was I?"

"Yes." His eyes crinkled a bit when he smiled, and he developed a fascinating groove in one cheek that was probably an old scar. "You were going to tell me how you came to live in New York because you are crazy about New York men. Especially tall ones."

She laughed a little. "Well, it's true. I did come here because of a man. He was a chef in the restaurant where I worked." She shrugged. "We fell in love, and I moved here with him. It didn't work out."

Bad news for the chef. Good news, he hoped, for Vince. "What happened?"

"He turned out not to be a good man," she said.

When Vince looked at her with pity, she said, "He got in with the wrong people. He got out of jail a couple of months ago."

"Has he bothered you?"

She shook her head. "He called, but I made it clear I won't see him. He is, as you Americans say, history."

"Good. Is there a man in your life now?"

She blinked. "Is there a particular reason you ask?"

Oh, how he could make her shiver with just a look. "Yes. I'd like to . . . get to know you better."

She rose and collected their plates. Vince also rose, and they cleared the table together. She went to the sink, and he moved her bodily out of the way. "You cooked. I'll wash up."

This was so . . . domestic that her heart gave a curious lurch.

She found a cloth and dried the dishes he washed. There was silence for a moment. Then he said, "Is that a problem for you?"

"You're a very direct man."

"Yes, ma'am. Clear, direct speaking is how I operate. I try to say what I mean and mean what I say. If more people did that, there'd be fewer problems in the world."

"But more hurt feelings, perhaps."

He grinned at that. "Well, I believe in direct speaking used judiciously, how's that?"

"Better."

"So, will you go out with me?"

"I'm not sure." She dried a plate so earnestly she nearly rubbed off the glaze before she realized what she was doing and placed it in the cupboard. "May I be as direct?"

"Of course."

She took a moment to compose what she wanted to ex-press. She wasn't one for blurting out exactly what she wanted—she wasn't used to hearing it done by others, either. On the other hand, she was drawn to this man with his big hands and his sweet, absurd dog, and his very straightforward manner.

"Come on," he said, "spit it out. If you're not interested, say so. I'll live."

"The last time I was this attracted to a man I ended up moving to a new country, learning a different language, and my lover ended up in jail. I'm . . . hesitant to get involved. And with a man I work for." There. She'd said it, and Vince himself couldn't have been more direct.

He pulled back a little, and she could see she'd surprised him. "Well, to take those points one at a time. I'm not asking you to change countries. We live in the same city. This seems to be a bilingual household. I stay within the law." He stepped closer. "I liked the part about you being attracted to me, though."

He took the tea towel out of her hands, flipped it over her head so it looped around her neck, and pulled her toward him.

"And the part about me working for you?" she asked a trifle breathlessly. He was close and she could feel the insidious pull of attraction much stronger than the pull of the tea towel.

"I promise that if this doesn't work out it won't affect your job."

She gazed at him, at his rugged, take-no-prisoners face and his sensuous eyes.

"Why don't we take this one step at a time?" he said, letting his lips whisper across hers. "Slow." He came back for another pass, adding a little pressure, his body touching hers lightly from chest to belly. "And easy." And he kissed her again, this time his lips settling on hers as though they meant to stay awhile.

She sighed into the kiss, slid into the easy warmth and pleasure of holding and being held.

New. She loved the new aspect of this man, all his secrets and mysteries yet to be revealed. What was he like as a lover? Which side of the bed did he sleep on? Was he grouchy in the morning? A shower Pavarotti?

She felt the thrill of sensation from her lips zipping all through her body, and she sensed that before long she'd be finding out the answers to all those questions.

Not quite yet, though.

She eased slowly back, knowing if she kissed him much longer, she'd be unable to pull away.

"Stay with me tonight," he said, his voice gruff with passion, his eyes dark and intense on hers.

"We only met yesterday."

"What does length of time have to do with it? Some things you know, instantly."

She understood what he meant, of course; she'd felt that strong and instant attraction, too, but she needed to think a little longer before moving to the next stage.

"You promised it would be slow and easy. I must go," she said.

"I'll drive you home."

"No. I can get a cab."

"Please let me drive you. Your knee . . ."

"All right. Thank you. And we can take Mimi out. Come, Mimi," she said briskly, pulling her attention away from Vince with an effort. The dog twirled and yipped with delight as her new lead was clipped to her new collar.

Vince took her hand as they left his apartment, and she didn't stop him.

It felt nice, his hand. Large and warm. As they left the building, her warm, fuzzy feeling was abruptly shattered. "Get out of here," they heard a man yell, followed by a familiar bark.

"Oh, no," she cried, seeing the dog who'd come to her and Mimi's aid being chased away by a burly man in jeans and a grimy T-shirt. She squeezed Vince's hand. "That's the dog who helped us."

"Hey, Bert. What's going on?" Vince said.

"God damned stray. I thought I'd got rid of it, but some asshole's been feeding the thing." He brandished the remains of the bone she'd given the dog herself.

"A stray?" she asked. "Are you sure he's a stray?"

"Course I'm sure. He hangs around, goes through the garbage. I called the pound couple times, but the bastard always runs away when he sees the truck."

"He's a beautiful dog, and so brave," she said. The Doberman loped up and put his nose against her side as if to say, "Can't you do something?"

He'd saved her and Mimi from goodness knew what. He was big and brave and sweet. There must be something she could do for him.

But as she was racking her brain for an answer, Mimi took matters into her own paws.

"Vince, look," Sophie said, laughing. Mimi was on her hind legs waving her two front paws at the big dog. "She plays coquette."

"That's great, lady. You hold on to him while I call the pound. The bastard won't get away this time."

"*Mais, non!*" she cried. "This dog must not go to the pound. He's a good dog. Brave and strong. He needs a home." She turned to Vince, who looked back at her, eyes narrowed in suspicion.

"I'm sure the animal shelter will find him a good home," he said.

Already she was stroking the dog in a way that looked far too much like an owner. "I wish I could have pets in my apartment, but it is not possible," she said, patting the dog's head the way she might have caressed a loved one on his way to the guillotine. "Look how well he and Mimi get on."

Vince felt a prickle of sweat form beneath where his hat band would sit if he were wearing a hat.

"If only you could take him while we try to find him a new home."

He knew where she was going with this, and it was vital he cut her off at the pass. "Sophie, I just got a dog." Though looking at Mimi, he knew that wasn't entirely true.

"Please, Vince, couldn't you give him a try? He's probably lost, and his owner is desperate to find him. I will put an ad in the paper and make posters to put in public places. Please?"

He stared down into eyes that were big and blue and full of appeal. He dropped his gaze to avoid saying yes to absolutely anything only to find two pairs of brown eyes staring up at him, as though they knew it was all up to him. He'd stared down angry teamsters, managed to hang tough in the face of threats ranging from legal action to physical violence, and he'd never wavered. But when Sophie looked at him with naked appeal in her eyes, he had trouble thinking, never mind saying no to her.

The Doberman had protected his girls when he hadn't been around to do it, and at least the Doberman looked like a dog, acted like a dog, and smelled like a dog; maybe he'd rub off on Mimi.

Still, Vince wasn't a pushover, and he was determined not to act like one.

He glared at the woman and the dog going dopey-eyed underneath her stroking hand—something he'd like to try sometime. "Is he house trained?"

"He's a very intelligent animal," she said in some indignation, but not answering the question.

"You want my opinion, you'll let the animal control people deal with him," the super said.

"No one asked for your opinion," Sophie said, indignation deepening her French accent.

A few more tense seconds passed before he gave in to the

inevitable. "All right," he said. "All right. But it's for a trial only. If that dog messes in the house or does anything I don't like, he goes to the pound. That is not negotiable."

She nodded, her eyes shining.

"All right," he said, knowing when he was beaten. "I'll take him in until we find him a home."

Of course, he was too evolved a man to hope that if he took in the dog at her request Sophie would be so grateful she'd sleep with him.

No, he realized, when she squealed with delight and kissed him full on the mouth, he wasn't evolved at all. He hoped she was grateful. Very, very grateful.

The super sent him a disgusted look as though Vince had let down the entire male gender.

With the scent of Sophie still in his nose and the taste of her on his lips, Vince didn't much care.

"Yer making a big mistake," the large guy said and stomped away. Mimi yapped at his retreating back, as though to say, "and don't come back."

The Doberman added a deep growl. "They're going to tag team us, aren't they?" Vince said to Sophie. "Tinkerbell and Godzilla."

"No," she assured him. "They'll be company for each other. It will be much better, I'm certain."

"They'll probably be terrible tonight, what with the Doberman settling in and everything. Probably it's too much for one person. You should definitely stay the night."

She smiled at him, the kind of smile that he bet went a lot of the way toward earning the sexy reputation French women enjoyed. "I'll sleep better knowing he's guarding you and Mimi," she said, and walked on, the Doberman trotting at her side.

Vince wasn't one to blow his own horn, but he had been a wrestling champ in college. He'd worked as a bouncer at a hot Manhattan club one summer. He did not need protection.

Unless it was from one much too sexy Frenchwoman who had somehow added another dog to his increasingly crowded life.

Three days ago he'd been a single man, living a bachelor existence in the greatest city in the world.

And since his aunt's funeral, his happy household of one had quadrupled. He looked at his three companions. One fourteen million dollar poodle, one very sexy French nanny who'd managed to get mugged, alienate his super, and saddle him with a homeless Doberman, and the stray mutt himself, who might or might not be house trained, not to mention dangerous or psychotic. There might be a very good reason why a dog known to have a fierce disposition was homeless. And yet, the Doberman had helped save Mimi and Sophie. Vince believed in returning a good deed with interest.

He sighed and fell in with the other three.

So, the four of them walked the block to where he garaged his vehicle and piled into his dusty SUV. The Doberman leaped into the back without a second's hesitation, but Mimi, naturally, wasn't a jump-in-the-back kind of dog. She sat on Sophie's lap the entire way as he headed south.

Sophie lived in an efficiency sublet in Greenwich Village, he learned. As he pulled up in front of a renovated town house, the kind that had been broken down into tiny apartments, he realized that he was well chaperoned. Getting invited up to her place was not going to be an option.

Perhaps that's why she suddenly stiffened and said, *"Oh, merde."* She'd turned her head and was looking out the window. He followed her gaze and saw a gaunt-looking man about his own age sitting on the red concrete steps.

"Problem?" he asked, his own hackles rising.

"Gregory." She sighed. "My ex." She sat there for another moment, then gave Mimi a kiss on top of her head, and reached for the door handle. "I'll see you in the morning."

Vince ignored her and got out of the car.

Gregory looked as though he didn't get out much. He was pale, and his eyes had the look of an angry, bitter man.

"What do you want?" Sophie asked when he rose from the steps to lounge against the black wrought-iron railing. Vince noticed that his expression transformed when he gazed at Sophie. He was obviously still in love with her.

"I want to talk to you."

She rubbed her arms. "Your probation officer called on Wednesday. You missed your appointment again."

He dropped his gaze and shuffled his feet on the cement step. A garbage truck roared by before he answered. "I was busy."

"You've got to stop seeing those men, Gregory. They'll only get you into more trouble."

"They're my friends," he insisted.

"Then I no longer am your friend." She shook her head sharply. "Don't come here again," she said, and hurried up the steps.

Her ex grabbed her arm as she tried to pass. "Let me come up and we can talk."

Vince had listened to enough. "Sophie told you to go."

"Yeah? And who the hell are you?"

"Her friend." He motioned behind him. "Get in the car and I'll drop you somewhere."

"Why don't you fuck off?"

Sophie was inside by this time, which was all he cared about. He trod deliberately up the stairs until he and the deadbeat ex were on a level. He had a good six inches on the guy and probably eighty pounds. "I look after my friends. I hear you've been anywhere near this street, and I'll be on you. Get it?"

Gregory exercised his impressive vocabulary by repeating his last line. Vince didn't move, simply pulled out his cell phone.

"Who are you calling?"

"The police. They might be interested in talking to you about rescheduling your appointment with your probation officer."

Gregory knocked the cell phone out of his hand and turned and ran.

Vince caught the phone and repocketed it, then hung around awhile before heading back home. He hadn't been able to protect her from getting knocked down today, but he could sure as hell keep the weasel chef away from her.

Sophie had been wrong about the dogs being company for each other. After he got them home, the Doberman launched himself on the pink princess bed and stretched full out as though unable to believe his luck. Vince did his best to encourage Mimi to shack up with her new buddy instead of him, but it was hopeless. She stayed in her princess bedroom while he was in there, but as soon as he went into his own room, he heard the click, click, click of her nails on the hardwood as she followed him, springing like an oversized flea onto his bed and heading straight for his feather pillow.

He was going to wake up in the morning smelling of Joy again. And not for the right reason.

Six

"Now that you have a love interest, we must update your image," Sophie said to Mimi the next day. "No, don't give me that pathetic look. We must speak English when Sir Galahad is around. It's all he understands."

Mimi whined, but Sophie was firm. "When I fell in love with an American, I learned English . . . Of course, that did not have a happy ending, but you may be luckier in love."

She put the leads on both dogs, delighted now that Vince had bought the leather and chain leash. Really, the man must be clairvoyant. He'd bought the perfect leash for Sir G the day before they met.

He was much more intuitive than he knew, that Vince.

"Now, I don't want to hurt your feelings, but you can't go around with blue hair and be considered au courant. The look was fine when you lived with old ladies, *naturellement,* but now you have Vince to think about, and the Doberman. You have to update, heh?"

Mimi looked unconvinced but trotted happily on one side of her, while Sir Galahad strained against his leash on her other side. "Look," she finally said in exasperation. "You are bigger. Your legs are longer, but Mimi can't keep up. She only has little legs. Now, you must behave."

After that it was better. She'd cancelled Mimi's standing hair appointment, deciding that any salon that would give a French poodle a blue rinse didn't need Mimi's business. Instead, they went to a place that Sophie herself patronized. It was run by an ex-patriot Frenchman who was brilliant with scissors. Most of the salon's staff had learned their craft in Paris.

Mimi was in her element. Surrounded by French people who cooed and fussed over her, she made no protest when her fur was colored back to white.

"I don't suppose . . ." Sophie gestured vaguely to where the Doberman stood with his nose against the door, leaving a big slobber mark on the glass.

"Sophie, *mon ange,* you know I love you, but the poodle is a fellow countryman, and *certainement* one helps one's own. The Doberman can go to the dog groomer around the corner."

Since there was a dog groomer nearby, Sophie was happy not to argue the point.

The Doberman, however, was less than happy when he reached his destination, but since they stocked dog cookies and bribed him freely, he consented to be washed and brushed. And defleaed.

While he was being groomed, she went back to Mimi and decided she looked so pretty when she was white again that her manicure needed redoing. They decided on a pale pink, and Sophie opted for the same shade herself.

That done, they picked up the other dog and walked home via the butcher so she could buy some filet mignon for the dogs, and a T-bone steak for Vince. "Because he has been very good to us, and we want to give him something a little special." She decided to buy some wine to go with the beef-steak, added some green beans from the greengrocer and tiny potatoes.

On their return, the Doberman again began to pull on the lead, and, since she wanted time to cook and for the wine to breathe, she picked Mimi up and hurried along. She stopped to shift the combined weights of Mimi, the groceries, the wine, and the straining Doberman when she heard a sound like popcorn popping. *Pop, pop, pop.* There was a thud as something hit the tree behind her and then she felt a sharp pinch in her upper arm. For a crazy second she thought she'd been shot, then noticed a thick splinter of wood had scratched her skin. A piece of tree bark clung to the cut which was bleeding slightly.

"*Mon Dieu,*" she cried. Moving on instinct rather than conscious intent, she huddled Mimi closer and pulled them all around to the other side of the tree. It wasn't much of a refuge, but it gave her a moment to take in the fact that she'd been shot at. Her arm burned a little where the bark chip had scratched her, but she didn't even want to think how much worse she'd feel if the bullet actually hit her instead of the tree.

She fumbled in her bag, praying she could get to the cell phone before the gunman got another crack at her.

"Are you all right?"

She'd never been so happy to hear the sound of another human voice. A middle-aged woman with what looked like twin Spaniels ran to her side, pulled the cell phone out of Sophie's trembling grasp, and called 9-1-1.

"Hold still, dear," the woman said, chattering to her that she'd learned first aid when her second husband developed heart problems. "He'd stop breathing, you see, and I had to learn to bring him back." While she chatted, she eased the splinter out of Sophie's arm and pressed a handkerchief—which she assured Sophie was clean—against the trickle of blood. Sophie's uppermost thought was that she'd been lucky enough to be hurt when possibly the only woman in New York who still used cotton handkerchiefs was in the vicinity.

Mimi trembled in her arms, or maybe it was her own trembling making the dog wobble, but Sir Galahad once more lived up to his name. Every hair on his body bristling, he stalked back and forth in front of them, a canine terminator.

Within a gratifyingly short time she heard the familiar peal of a siren. Before they arrived, she made a second call. To Vince. She suspected he was going to fire her. So far, in her short employment with him, she'd run into disaster twice.

But, contrary to her expectations, he wasn't upset with her, but frantic over her safety.

He acted a lot like the Doberman when he got home less than half an hour after she called. Having given a statement to the police, and refused a ride to the hospital, she was sitting with her feet up, Mimi curled in her lap and Sir Galahad pacing in front of the door ready to attack anyone who came after them. Sophie had the oddest feeling that he was chagrined not to have prevented her injury earlier.

The Doberman growled deep in his throat before she heard anything. Instinctively, she grabbed Mimi tighter, then relaxed when the I'm-a-guard-dog-mess-with-me-at-your-peril growling changed to a puppyish whine and the dog wagged its stub of a tail.

Vince was home. She let out her breath and loosened her viselike grip on poor Mimi. Somehow she felt that everything would be okay.

Vince was so big and tough that her tension left her when he roared through the door with an absent pat for Sir Galahad and eyes only for her.

"Why aren't you in the hospital?" were his first words.

"There's no need."

"I came as fast as I could. My God, you could have been killed."

As he spoke, he crossed the room in a couple of fast strides and dropped to his knees beside her chair, studying the bandage a paramedic had applied.

"I'm fine. Really. It's just a graze."

"You were attacked. You are not fine." He touched her hand, her face, as though he could impart his strength to her. "You're pale."

"I had a shock," she admitted. "I'm so sorry."

"That bastard." Vince jumped to his feet. "I hope you're pressing charges."

"What are you talking about?"

"That pissant who wants you back."

"You mean Gregory?" In truth, she'd never considered him as the one who'd shot at her.

"You were mugged yesterday; he's hanging around your place when you get home, where you tell him to piss off. Then you get shot at today. Don't you think that's a bit of a coincidence?"

"This is New York."

He did not look convinced, and she began to wonder. Was it possible? Gregory was a man of weak character, as she'd discovered too late, but would he try to hurt her? It was hard to believe. It was tough to think at all when her arm felt as if it had been burned, and her head ached.

Vince began to pace, a little like the Doberman had earlier. In fact, Sir Galahad was now lying across the door, as though he'd given over the pacing part of the job to Vince.

"You're not going home," Vince said at last.

"I'm not?"

"No. You're staying here for a few days. I'll take some time off work, and we'll figure out what's going on."

"I thought you were going to fire me," she said.

He sent her an impatient glance. "Don't be stupid. He wouldn't be going after you if he didn't sense I'm interested in you. This is my fault."

She knew there were problems with Vince's logic, but right now she didn't feel like working them out. All she wanted to do was lie down.

She couldn't quite work up the energy to argue, but she tried. "My things . . ."

"We'll go later and get them." He looked down at her, and his hard face softened. "You need some painkillers and some sleep."

"I can't share your bed," she managed.

"Then you can share Mimi's." And without another word, he put a strong arm behind her shoulders and another beneath her knees, then scooped her up with great gentleness.

"But for today, you can nap in my bed. It's bigger."

So she found herself in moments tucked into his big, big bed, with the scent of Vince comforting her. He brought her a glass of water and a bottle of extra-strength painkillers. He shook out two which she swallowed, then lay down. A moment later she felt the bedcovers give, and the fluffy coat of Mimi brushed her hand. She smiled and drifted into sleep.

Vince called a buddy, Ed, who just happened to be a cop, and told him of his suspicions. Sophie's ex wasn't going to get another chance to hurt her. Vince couldn't imagine a man sick enough to try to shoot a woman to keep her out of the arms of another man, but he had to admit that Sophie was the kind of woman who inspired the grand gesture.

Here he was in the middle of a tricky negotiation, and he'd just walked away to take a few days off. No explanation. No definite return date. But right now the safety of a woman he'd already come to care for rated a lot higher on his list of priorities than whether the latest union shop with a grievance got a four percent increase instead of two and an end to contracting out of services.

Vince made his living on this stuff. Normally he'd be salivating over the two percent difference, loving the working guys with their straight-up talk, and the management position, which predictably complained that the company could no longer be profitable with that kind of raise.

There was always a solution, always an answer that pleased neither side but was acceptable to both, and Vince was the man who could instinctively find the delicate balance point between the two.

But not this week.

Not when he was worried sick about Sophie and wanting to take apart the asshole ex who was trying to hurt her.

Seven

Sophie woke with a start, sitting up in bed before she realized she was no longer asleep. The silky bedspread sighed as she shifted.

Something had awakened her.

What?

In a second she had the answer.

Yap, yap, yap . . . and the scrabbling of sharp nails across hardwood.

Mimi.

Sophie threw off the covers and had her feet planted on the floor before she was conscious that she was awake.

Mimi might be a little on the ditzy side even for a poodle, but she had sharp ears and a terrific sense of self-preservation. Sophie was out in the hall in seconds.

As she careened through the doorway, grabbing the only weapon she could find—a scrubby-looking baseball bat with a few scrawled signatures on it, she saw Mimi was doing her pit bull imitation. Her dainty snout was pulled back in a snarl, her little body almost comically fierce as she attacked the door, barking, barking, barking, her freshly manicured nails sliding and clacking as she menaced the unknown enemy on the other side of the door.

Even as she took in the sight of Mimi, Sophie became aware of Vince flying out of his own room. His weapon of choice wasn't a baseball bat but a lethal-looking hand gun.

In her time in America, Sophie had still never become used to the prevalence of guns. This one was gray black. She didn't have to ask if it was loaded. Vince's expression of deadly earnest told her it was.

"Get back in your room, Sophie," he said, barely glancing her way. Three nights she'd slept in the Princess bed, and nothing had happened. Vince had insisted she remain, for her own safety, and she'd let him talk her into staying for several reasons, most of which had nothing to do with her safety; but maybe he was right.

She ignored his order, of course, feeling that they needed to work as a team if they were to thwart whatever danger lurked outside.

Besides, she couldn't have moved if she'd tried. Vince looked *incroyable* in his clothes, but wearing nothing but a pair of faded navy cotton boxer shorts, *Mon Dieu*.

He was tall and broad; that much she'd known with his clothes on. What she hadn't known was that one look at his chest would make her want to bury her face in the triangle of brown, silky-looking hair and sink her teeth not entirely gently into his nipples.

She hadn't imagined his belly would be rock hard and ridged with muscle, or that his legs would be elegant in spite of the big muscles.

She hadn't imagined she could want a man so much when she knew so little about him. Yes, he was right, on the most personal level, she should run back into her bedroom and slam the door.

But what if she and her oh-so-American baseball bat were needed?

For a tense moment they stayed that way. She with her bat raised, heat from her nervous palm making the handle slippery, Vince with a calm expression of concentration on his face as he pointed his awful gun at the door, and Mimi, all animation and aggression, doing her best to imitate a canine army.

The last roommate to wander into the melee was the Doberman. He yawned, padded on long legs to the door, sniffed, and looked down at Mimi from his superior height, as though to say, "Why the hysterics?"

Down the hall, a door shut. Someone had come home late.

Mimi, seeming to bow to Sir Galahad's superior guard dog instincts, tried to explain her error with little yaps, some pawing of the air, and a general batting of eyelashes and tossing of fluffy head.

Sir Galahad sat and scratched his ear.

She rose to her hind legs and twirled.

Sophie had to smile.

The Doberman was more severe. He sniffed under the door, snorted, gave one deep-throated woof and padded back to bed, Mimi, still explaining, following him on short, exquisitely coiffed legs.

Vince was taking no chances, Sophie realized, when he approached the door, checked the peephole, applied the chain, and opened the door.

"Nothing," he said in his deep, slow voice as he closed and locked the door once again. "Damn dog."

"She's on edge. We all are," Sophie said, eager to justify Mimi's actions.

"Maybe," Vince said, and clicking the safety on his gun, walked slowly toward her.

Sophie refused to back up as he advanced on her in nothing but a pair of boxers that really didn't hide all that much. But she couldn't stop her heart picking up speed or her skin going twitchy as Vince closed in on her. He was all drowsy masculinity and awakening sexuality.

Her own desire bumped to life as he stopped in front of her, looking down into her eyes with sleepy amusement and carnal intent flickering. "Unless you're trying to get a game of scrub going, I think we can dispense with the baseball bat."

She allowed him to take it from her and prop it against the wall. He approached her once again, awfully light-footed for such a big man.

"Unless you're planning on playing Russian roulette?" She indicated the gun still in his hand.

He glanced at it as though he'd forgotten it was there and said, "I'll put this back in my bedroom."

"I'll say good night, then," she said, taking a step backward.

He eyed her, a warm, devilish glint in his eyes making her aware of how short her gown was and that the excitement or change of temperature perhaps had caused her nipples to pop out and see what was going on.

The air tingled with possibilities.

He said, "You got out here pretty fast. Weren't you asleep?"

She'd been lying there listening to the Doberman snore, her body on fire for the man in the other room. No, she hadn't been sleeping. She shook her head, realizing he'd roared into the hall almost at the same moment she had. And he hadn't looked like a man woken from deep sleep, either.

She sent him a questioning look.

Got back a rueful grin. "This is crazy. If we both can't sleep, I can think of something else I'd rather be doing."

Her heart, which had barely calmed after the recent scare, began to race again. "And what is that?"

"Come on and I'll show you."

He didn't say another word, simply took her wrist and pulled her along with him.

She could have pulled away; she could have said, *non, merci*. She could simply have stopped in her tracks. But she didn't do any of those things. She acted as though her wrist was welded to his hand and she had no choice but to follow.

She was aware of everything about the moment: The way

her short gown brushed her thighs as they walked, the comparative silence of New York in the middle of the night—the traffic sounds diminished to a rumble, a siren wailing somewhere. The feel of bare feet on hardwood, the cool night air on her arms, the heat in her wrist where Vince held her. She saw him dimly ahead of her, a big, forceful shape. Solid, reliable; a man a woman could turn to in a crisis.

A man who made a woman feel small and dainty and feminine.

They entered Vince's bedroom. He kept walking until he reached the side of the bed, then without releasing her, pulled open the drawer on his bedside table. The gun made an unpleasant thunk as it landed inside, and she was glad when Vince slid the drawer shut on the thing.

He straightened and turned toward her then, and she felt every cell in her body snap to full alert. Dawn filtered smudgy light into the room, so the man standing before her seemed like solid shadow, dark and mysterious.

He took a moment simply to gaze down at her; then he raised his free hand and traced an eyebrow, as though it were the first feature he'd noticed. Next he touched her cheek, her lips, her chin, and suddenly her wrist was free as he brought one hand to her hip and the other slid from her chin, followed the line of her jaw, and slipped to cup the back of her neck.

There was probably an inch separating them, and she felt the back-and-forth current of desire pulling them inevitably together. His head came down slowly, and she raised her face to receive his kiss.

His lips touched hers—warm, and firm, and surprisingly gentle, and yet she felt the power within them, within him. His hands touched her lightly, but the echo of great strength was in the soft brush of his palm against her skin.

He held himself in check, and she liked him for it. She took pleasure from the banked promises in his quiet kiss and slow-moving hands.

She enjoyed American men with their cleanliness and crisp edges, but this one combined the earthy sensuality of the Frenchman. The best of both worlds, she thought as she sighed and molded her body to his, so they touched, her breasts to his chest, his erection rubbing at her belly.

He deepened the kiss, and she tasted the faint mint of his toothpaste, and the hot taste of aroused male.

He smelled of the Ivory soap she'd seen in his bathroom, of the herb shampoo she'd uncapped and sniffed when her curiosity about him had surfaced.

She heard him sigh, heard herself murmur some nonsense that wasn't French or English, but a muddled mixture of the two.

He licked at her, toyed with her mouth, seemed happy to make up for the hours of sleep they'd both missed by spending as many hours again standing here kissing her while dawn tracked its slow way toward full day.

Vince seemed fascinated by every detail of her. Having kissed her mouth until a drumbeat of heavy desire built, thudding inside her with a steadily increasing tempo, he traced the muscles and bone of her back through the slippery silk of her nightgown. He cupped her hips in his big hands and explored her body through her clothing.

She ran her hands down the front of his body, letting her fingers slip through the coarse hair on his chest. She toyed with the bumps of nipple, hit the smooth warmth and surprisingly silky slide of skin below his rib cage, then slipped her hand into the waistband of his boxers to find him hot and oh, so very . . . She searched her English vocabulary for the correct word. *Enorme. Magnifique.* Imposing. Yes, she liked that word. A good English word. Imposing.

He felt so good when she curled her fingers around him. She squeezed lightly, and there was no give. He was like warm, smoothly polished granite.

She played with him until he cursed softly, his feet shifting like a stallion about to race, and suddenly he was yanking her nightgown up and over her head.

Panting. They were both panting.

She felt the relative coolness of air against her skin like a wave as he pulled the gown over her head.

The wisp of silk floated to the floor, and by the time it landed, Vince had shucked his boxers and tossed them much less ceremoniously to the ground.

A shiver of anticipation danced over her bare skin. What would he be like? Feel like? Taste like? Now they were relative strangers; soon they'd be as intimate as a man and woman could be. She was dying to get on with it even as she wanted to stretch out this moment of anticipation.

The moment was soon gone, however. Vince pulled her against him and started touching her naked body, bending down to kiss her. When their height differences frustrated him, he scooped her up with thrilling machismo and laid her on his bed. His big bed where she'd napped, and where the scent of him clung to the bedding.

"You're so small," he said in a voice of wonder, running his hands down her body. Actually, he was the one who was big. Everywhere.

A tiny doubt niggled at her that she'd be able to accommodate him inside her body, but she did her best to quell it. She was a Frenchwoman, after all. The blood of the greatest courtesans and mistresses in history ran through her veins. She'd yet to meet the man who was too much for her—in any way.

She was delicate boned, but on the tall side for a woman, at five feet, seven inches. In France, men tended to be built on a smaller scale, so she was accustomed to feeling tall. But Vince dwarfed her and made her feel tiny and dainty.

When she snuggled up against him, she fit her mouth to his mouth, breast to his chest, and ended up with the hot pressing length of him against her belly. Her feet ended not far past his knees.

As he touched her, he talked. Silly, foolish statements. "You have a swimmer's muscles." He was right, she did. "Your skin's so soft." Oh, and the way he was stroking it, she'd soon be purring. "Your nipples taste so good." Which was nothing on how his mouth and tongue felt against her sensitive skin.

She didn't know a lot of men who talked in bed, but it was a nice quality, she decided. She liked the brush of warm air touching her skin when he spoke against it. Enjoyed the earthy praise he scattered along with his kisses.

"You're so slight, I can count your ribs." Then he did. Kissing the lowest one and running his tongue along the ridge of bone. "One," he muttered, then climbed to the next rib, "Two," and so on until he was licking the underside of her breast, and he'd muddled his counting dreadfully.

When he shifted so he was between her thighs, she opened for him, spreading herself wide both physically and emotionally. That's how she was about sex. It was never just physical for her, and sometimes it didn't work out and there was pain afterward, but oh, the pleasure in between.

So, she opened herself completely, and he entered her slowly, as though making love with her this first time was something he wanted to remember forever. The sky lightened a little more, and a streak of pink lit up the room so she saw the planes of his face more clearly, the dark gleam of his eyes, watching her.

Then he began to move. Slow at first, and so careful of her as their passion built quietly, until she needed more friction, more speed. She grabbed his hips, digging her fingers into the wonderful tight muscles of his butt and pulling him into her, increasing the rhythm until they were both breathing hard and a drop of warm sweat hit her cheek.

"Oh, you feel so good."

"Yes. Oh, yes." She felt very, very good. And then better, and then impossibly, wonderfully, heart-stirringly oh, *Mon Dieu!* as she cried out and shattered.

One more long, beautiful thrust inside her pulsing body,

another, causing tiny aftershocks to radiate deep within her; he wanted to hold himself back, she could tell, just as she knew he couldn't hold on much longer. His cry was guttural and fierce when he exploded deep within her body. She held him through his shudders, loving the feel of his muscles and skin so damp and hot rubbing against hers.

They kissed and held each other for a long time and then fell asleep just as day was breaking.

Vince woke to silence. He took a moment to stretch and orient himself. A smug grin was plastered across his face where he suspected it would stay for days.

He reached out for Sophie, as he'd reached for her twice more during their few hours together, each time finding her sleepily responsive, and then wildly so. But the grin stalled when he realized he was alone in the bed. A glance at the clock told him it was ten-thirty. Late for him to start the day, but then, he hadn't exactly had a restful night.

Probably, she was making coffee, and breakfast, he thought as he rolled to his back and contemplated all the wonders of a gorgeous, sexy, Cordon Bleu-trained dog sitter staying in his apartment.

He sniffed appreciatively, wondering what the chances were that she'd bring him the paper in bed. Hmm. Maybe the Doberman could be trained to fetch the *Times* and bring it to him on the weekends. He sniffed again . . . but none of the mouth-watering smells from his fantasy were reaching him. No rich, dark coffee aroma, no scent of sizzling bacon.

It was so quiet he might as well be alone in the apartment. He didn't hear a single dog sound. No scratching at his door, no snuffling, no clicking nails on his hardwood floors, no howling, growling, barking of any kind.

He was out of bed and dragging on jeans in an instant.

"Sophie?" he called out as he yanked open the bedroom door.

Nothing.

Even more odd, no clatter of tiny and oversized paws flying hell for leather across the floor to maul him. Only silence. Eerie, heart-pounding silence.

Sophie was gone. The dogs were gone. He took a second to regroup and try to calm his pounding heart when it registered on his panicked brain that the leashes were also gone.

She'd taken off for a walk.

Panic turned to anger.

What was the matter with the woman? A crazy ex was stalking her and taking pot shots, and she was going back out there on foot. Did she have a death wish?

He was out of his front door and pounding down the hallway when he heard the elevator doors open, and there she was, looking as fresh as a spring morning, with Lady and The Tramp in tow, a brown bag from which heavenly fresh-bread scents arose, and a smile that had his heart pounding all over again. Instead of blasting off at her as he'd planned, he felt more like the Doberman, who gazed at her adoringly and drooled.

"Good morning," she said, in a soft, sexy tone that reminded him of every intimate thing they'd done last night. Her accent was as soft and alluring as a caress. When she spoke he heard the slide of cotton bedsheets across heated, tangled limbs, the pant and sigh and "oh, that feels so good" of great sex.

It was there in her sparkling eyes and knowing smile, the way he could see her nipples perk to attention flirtatiously as she gazed at him, so he felt his cock stand to attention ready to flirt back. More than flirt.

He couldn't blast her, and he couldn't stand here in the hall with his tongue hanging out about to whine softly for a treat. He had something important to say, and he had to say it.

"You should have woken me," he managed.

Her smile curved higher. "You need your sleep. For later."

His lips turned to rubber. Not later, he wanted to say.

Now. "I was worried." And in that second he realized how absurd it was to stand out in the hallway with the still-leashed dogs staring raptly up at the pair of them. The Dob sat, alert, as though at any moment a Frisbee was going to go sailing down the hall and he had to be ready to fly after it. Mimi was fully reclined, her head resting on her ridiculous manicured paws, only her beady black eyes following the conversation, her pom-pom tail wagging softly when she heard their voices.

Instantly, Sophie's eyes flashed sympathy. "Oh, Vince. I am so sorry. I did not think. I only went to the French bakery. Come. I will make us some coffee, and you may scold me all you please."

She bustled past him, her hands full of dog leashes and paper sack, trailing an illusive fragrance that made him want to get her naked ASAP.

Pulling himself together with an effort, he followed her into his apartment and to the kitchen. Refusing to act like some boorish brute who let the little woman do everything, he got the coffee started while she put bread, cheeses, and jam on the table. Not to be outdone, he pulled out his plastic squeeze bottle of honey in the shape of a bear. She fussed a little with dishes and napkins. Sliced melon and rinsed fresh strawberries. Put on a CD that one of his old girlfriends had left behind. One of those female crooners with a single bizarre name. Dido, maybe. Or Enya.

Once they were sitting and he'd poured them both coffee, he took a good hit of caffeine to get his brain in gear.

"Look, Sophie." He reached across and took her hand, was about to say, "You can't do that; you can't go out without telling me," when she leaned forward, squeezing his fingers with her own.

"I had a wonderful time last night."

Boom, there it went again, any sensible thought. He'd always thought the idea of a woman blowing a man's mind was a figment of songwriters' imaginations or teenage boys with crushes. But nope. Here he was, a thirty-four-year-old man with his mind blown clean of all rational thought.

Except the completely rational urge to be intimate with this fascinating woman. Nothing could keep the answering grin off his face. "I had a fantastic time, too." It was almost scary how good he felt this morning. Which only made her safety that much more vital to preserve.

"But here's the thing. You can't go out like that without telling me."

A tiny frown appeared between her brows. "But I have to. The dogs must be walked. I must shop for food."

"I'll walk the dogs until we have that bastard back behind bars." And if Vince could arrange a half hour or so with Sophie's insane stalking ex before the police nabbed him, he'd remind him that it was a very bad idea to mess with Sophie anymore.

Her frown deepened as she looked at him. Absently, she rubbed the spot where the wood chip had grazed her. "I can't believe Gregory would shoot at me. It doesn't seem like him."

"I know, honey. I'm sorry. I've got some friends who are cops. I've already called my buddy Ed. They'll get him soon, I promise. But until they do you have to stay here and be safe."

She pulled her hand away and reached for a slice of baguette, still warm from the bakery. "I must shop," she reminded him.

"We'll go together," he said. "We can buy in bulk, enough food for a few weeks."

Her nostrils flared as she made an expression of disgust. "Shop in bulk? One does not buy good, fresh food in a warehouse, Vincent. I cannot work this way."

A jug of wine, a stack of frozen Hungry Man dinners, and thou would do fine for Vince, but he had a pretty good idea she wouldn't feel that way.

Food kept you alive. Why did she have to go and make it an art form? "You can give me a list of things. I'll get them fresh."

"But I am supposed to be the caregiver. You can't do my work."

"I think after last night we've moved to a different level. Please. I can't let anything happen to you."

"But I'll be like a prisoner. I can't live like that." She rose suddenly, walked to his phone, and lifted the receiver.

What was she doing? Calling a cab? Cold sweat prickled at his neck. She couldn't go like this; how could he protect her?

"Who are you phoning?"

"Gregory."

He rose, too. "You can't call him. Are you insane? He's trying to kill you."

She flapped her hand at him in a classic *shut up* move. He thought about yanking the phone out of the wall, but retained enough sense to realize that acting like a barbarian wasn't going to reassure her about staying in his apartment 24/7. So he waited in frustrated silence for a few minutes.

Her shoulders slumped after a minute, and she replaced the phone. "He doesn't answer. The answer machine is not on." She flicked a glance his way, and he knew he'd convinced her, at least halfway. If her insane ex wasn't answering the phone at his place, then where the hell was he?

Vince strode to the window and looked out, but no lunatic wearing a chef's hat and brandishing a shotgun appeared to be hanging out down at street level. Still, he was glad he had a gun of his own, and at least one dog he could count on in a crisis. He forced himself to relax and turned back to Sophie. "Let's eat our breakfast," he said.

She nodded, but somehow the warm intimacy of earlier was gone.

A stalker with a gun was hell on a budding romance.

Eight

"What are we going to do, then, stuck here all day?"

"I have a few ideas."

"We can't make love all day," she said, shaking her head so her dark hair brushed her jaw and gesticulating with her hands, including the one that held bread spread with strawberry jam.

In her agitation, she waved the bread about, and a dollop of jam toppled off the bread to land on her shirt, where it covered the upper slope of her right breast.

"*Merde!*" she cried, dropping the bread on her plate and picking up a napkin. He watched the jam, fascinated. It caught the light when she moved and glowed ruby. He took the napkin from her and said, "Let me."

He leaned forward. He watched her breasts rise and fall as she breathed, watched the patch of preserves. The scent of strawberry was as sweet as summer. He put his lips to the spot and sucked the jam into his mouth.

She laughed. "What are you doing?"

"I'm cleaning you up. I like to do a very thorough job," he promised her. He was thinking he'd get her mind off her troubles for a while, but the minute he got close to her, he was lost.

He looked down, and where he'd pulled part of her cotton shirt into his mouth, he'd left a crinkly round wet spot. There was still a little jam left, so he leaned forward and this time pulled more shirt into his mouth, and sneaky devil that he was, he managed to get her nipple this time.

There was some kind of flimsy bra there as well, but he still made the most of his position, using his teeth gently but firmly to be sure she felt him through all that fabric. She sighed and pushed forward against him, grabbing the back of his head and pulling him tighter against that wonderful round flesh. He smelled her laundry soap, and her skin, and strawberries.

He launched himself at the other breast until he'd made another patch of wet blouse and bra, and another nipple was hard on his tongue.

When he pulled back, he was breathing heavily, and so was she. Sunlight spilled through the window, tossing bars of light across the sturdy pine table, the food, and the woman laughing at him breathlessly. Suddenly, he was filled with a lust so strong it was more need than desire.

"I want you," he said.

"I know." And she did. He could see his own desire reflecting back from her. Beneath the wet patches on her shirt her nipples were rock hard in the wet, wrinkled fabric—almost shocking against the elegant and unmussed rest of her.

He scooted closer and kissed her mouth, thrusting his tongue deep in his frantic need. She licked at him, nipped him, took over his mouth as he made short work of the buttons down her front. He managed her bra by feel, then kissed his way down to her still-damp breasts, the centers puckered and her beautiful, sensitive, coral-tipped nipples luring him until he took one into his mouth.

It wasn't enough. It didn't seem like anything could ever be enough with this woman. He wanted all of her, now. His hands were under her skirt, reaching. She gripped the seat and lifted her hips so he could strip off her panties.

Crazed with lust, he stood and shoved their breakfast to one end of the table. He heard a thunk as something crashed to the floor, but he didn't much care. In the other room one of the dogs let out one muffled bark at the sound, but neither came to investigate for which he was grateful. He didn't want a crowd watching what he was about to do.

He pulled Sophie from her seat and hoisted her to the edge of the table. She clung to his shoulders, reaching up so she could kiss him again. He could taste her urgency, feel her mounting desire, and it fueled his own. Or his fueled hers.

He bunched her skirt around her hips, then decided he needed her to be naked. So he took the extra few seconds to strip her of her skirt and then pushed her gently to her back until she was laid out on his table like a feast. Her skin was honey-toned in the warm light, her nipples dark coral. As she drew in a shuddering breath, he watched her rib cage rise, then the slight swell of her belly.

She was surrounded by the remains of their breakfast. The fruit, some bread, the jam, his squeeze bottle of honey . . .

As he reached across her, she reminded him he was fully dressed still by grabbing his T-shirt and pulling.

One hand on the honey, the other reaching behind him, he yanked the thing over his head, put down the honey beside her raised knee, and then slipped the shirt off his arms.

Sophie rose to her elbows and without a word looked significantly toward his crotch. Some things could be communicated in any language, he realized, as he obligingly stripped out of the clothes he'd dressed in less than an hour ago.

He stepped between her knees, thought about parting them, then looked down at her, so glorious, the dark triangle of hair in the shadow cast by her raised legs. He wanted the sun on it.

"Open yourself for me," he said softly.

A tiny sound came from her throat. For a second she didn't move, and then she parted her knees with enough slowness to torture them both.

"All the way," he whispered, waiting until her thighs rested on the table, her knees hanging over. The sun turned her hair glossy, her thighs impossibly pale. He could see the faint line of a blue vein and followed it higher to where she was glistening with her own desire. Wet and plump and so very open for him.

If he went down on her now, which he wanted to do quite desperately, it would all be over far too quickly. He wanted to draw out their pleasure. So he picked up his bear-shaped squeeze bottle of honey, leaned right over her, and squirted a golden drizzle onto her right nipple, then drew a lazy line to her left.

"It feels cold," she gasped, when he trailed the honey down, between her ribs, across her belly, filling her belly button with a golden pool of honey. Where he drizzled the honey goose bumps sprang up. He thought it the most erotic sight. He stopped just below her navel, and her hips jerked a little, in frustration, he guessed. Good. He wanted her on edge.

At least as on edge as he was himself.

Back to her breasts, and he licked at the honey, swirled it around with his tongue, rubbed his lips until they were smothered with it, and kissed her mouth, covering her with sticky sweetness. He lapped at her lips, making her giggle, lapped his way back to her breasts, and tongued her until he no longer tasted sweetness, then continued to follow the sweet path he'd drawn. As he tracked his way south, her body began to tremble, and her sighs turned into quick pants.

As he dipped his tongue into her navel, he saw her hands grip the sides of the table. She never closed her legs, though. She kept herself completely open to him, and he loved her for it.

Her eyes were tightly closed so she never noticed when he picked up the honey bottle again. As he drizzled the thick, golden liquid into her curls and over her pulsing clit, she cried out.

She was wet, and sweet and sticky. Her own musky scent mingled with the honey, and he salivated as he closed in on her. The minute his tongue touched her she cried out. He felt the shudders already beginning; her intimate flesh was plump and sweet with her desire. As much as he wanted to make this last for both of them, she was too close, and he couldn't hold himself back. He lapped at her gently, until she tipped her hips up and pushed against him. Then he cupped her hips in his big hands and licked and sucked greedily. Her panting was growing harsh, her own wetness outpacing the honey, and then, when neither of them could wait another second, he sucked her clit into his mouth and tongued her hard.

A cry seemed torn from her as she climaxed against his mouth. Her torso rose as though she were climbing a rope— literally trying to climb out of her own skin, he thought smugly.

He heard another *Mon Dieu* and then a lot of other stuff that sounded earthy and exactly the kind of thing a woman should say in the throes of orgasm. Especially as he caught his own name in there.

He kissed his way back up her body, leaving sticky honey mixed with essence-of-Sophie lip prints along the way. When they kissed, she wrapped herself around him, pushing herself up so they ended with her sitting on the edge of the table, her legs wrapped around his hips. She was still hot and wet, and he felt the little aftershocks against his own needy nakedness.

A small, firm hand grasped his shaft and guided him to the opening of her body. Once more he cupped her hips. She clung to his neck, and they never stopped kissing as he thrust, hard and deep inside her.

Oh, she was so exquisitely, absolutely right. Tight and wet and so very hot. He was pumping, she was pumping, their tongues were mating, the honey was doing its best to seal them together, and then suddenly her head fell back. He wondered for a second if he'd deprived her of so much oxygen she'd passed out, but she drew in a great shuddering breath, and then he got it. Her lower body clenched him as she used that breath to cry out her release. He managed to get her all the way through her climax, while his cock felt like pure fire. He couldn't hold on, couldn't hold it, and suddenly it didn't matter; the fire poured out of him, into her while he shuddered his heart out.

He found that his legs were trembling, so he had to hold on to the edge of the table for support. He dropped his head to her shoulder and kissed the damp, soft skin of her neck.

Then, because he felt like it, he lifted her, still joined to him and walked them both into his shower. He'd never been so glad that he'd renovated the bathroom to suit his oversized frame.

Between the shower, her begging him to let her cook him the world's most complicated meal, more sex, and time to sit and talk, the hours passed. If her safety was never far from his mind, he didn't let on, and Sophie never once made noises about leaving his apartment.

She even decided to trust him with her shopping list, sort of.

"I must have some moules," Sophie decided suddenly. She'd begun making noises about dinner, and rude comments about his lack of kitchen supplies. She glanced at him sternly.

"Mules?" he asked, wondering if she meant those girlie slippers with heels. He hoped she didn't mean the beasts of burden. That's all he needed in the apartment, more animals.

"Moules, mussels." She made a sharp gesture, a flick of her wrist, and an opening of the fingers. "And they must be fresh."

He blinked at her.

"For dinner. Yes? You like mussels?"

He had a feeling she could cook road kill and make it taste delicious. Or mules.

She opened cupboards and started muttering to herself in French. Mimi wagged her tail at the sound and sighed daintily through her black button nose.

While Sophie wrote him a list that included a separate list of ingredients for the dogs' dinner, he collected leashes and decided to take the dogs with him.

While Mimi and the Doberman did their thing, he kept a sharp eye out for trouble, but his neighborhood seemed as peaceful as it ever did. He got everything on her list, including the mussels which he was assured twice were fresh.

He returned, and things went fine until Sophie, in the middle of cooking dinner, suddenly said, "You have no cardamom."

He felt like saying, *well, duh.* Vince considered himself a liberal-minded man, but he secretly suspected that a single guy who stocked cardamom, whatever the hell that was, also wore pink golf shirts and subscribed to *House and Home.*

Nothing wrong with that, of course, but Vince wasn't that sort of man. Mind you, he had to admit that a man who gave Mimi house room might as well grow a cardamom tree in his living room. If they grew on trees. Jeez.

While he harbored these reflections, Mimi snoozed on his favorite chair, and the Doberman sat at Sophie's feet watching the dinner preparations with unblinking brown eyes.

"Imbecile!" Sophie said, after she stepped backward and almost fell over the dog. *"Que tu es bête!"*

"He doesn't understand English," Vince said with deep appreciation as the dog wagged its tail while Sophie insulted it.

"He must move."

"Probably he's hungry."

"He's always hungry, this one."

"I think there are some dog cookies in the cupboard," Vince said. "They came with Mimi's things, but she won't touch them."

He moved around behind Sophie, giving her a wide berth, since he was not keen to be called imbecile and the like unless strictly necessary. He reached into a cupboard and brought out a seriously embarrassing looking can with hand-painted poodles all over it. A custom job, no doubt, like the collar. He eased open the lid, and inside were bone-shaped cookies that had to be handmade. Probably from some specialty poodle boutique.

He tossed one at the Doberman, who caught it in midair and wolfed it down. He tossed a second, and that went the way of the first. To be fair, he walked over to where Mimi snoozed and waved one under her nose. She didn't even open an eye, just scooched her body a bit so her nose moved farther away from the dog cookie.

"Finicky," Vince said, replacing the tin.

"Cardamom I must have," Sophie insisted. "I know where you can buy it."

"Yeah, well, so do I," Vince lied. "You keep cooking. I'll get it."

"Are you sure?" She looked doubtful.

"Sophie, I'm a college-educated man; I can manage to buy cinnamon."

"Cardamom!"

He grinned at her. "I know. I was joking."

She threw her hands in the air and started muttering. Sometimes, he decided a language barrier wasn't such a bad thing.

He glanced at the dogs, but they seemed engrossed in their various activities. Sleeping on *his* chair and supervising the dinner preparation. Seemed a shame to bother them. Besides, they'd be some protection for Sophie in his absence, and he'd be a lot less noticeable without them. If the insane chef was hanging around, he hoped to surprise him.

So he headed off alone. He checked out the perimeter of the building, and the adjacent areas, but everything seemed okay. It took him three stores to find cardamom. He was about to pick it up when his cell phone rang. It was Sophie, and she sounded frantic.

"Vince," she cried, "come quick."

Nine

He was already running, his steps keeping time with his pounding heart.

That bastard must have waited until he was out of the way to try to get to Sophie.

"I'm two minutes away," he yelled into the phone. "Did you call 9-1-1?"

"9-1-1? But they can't—"

"Whatever you do, don't let that bastard inside."

"Vincent, he's already inside. Oh, I must go to him. Hurry!"

The phone cut out, and he shut every distraction from his mind, focusing on only one goal. He had to save Sophie. She was alive, and somehow she'd been able to call him. She was smart and brave. If she could hold Gregory a couple more minutes, he'd be there. Sprinting up Eleventh Avenue, he bashed a few shoulders, leaped over a couple of dogs on leashes, and nearly lost an arm when he dodged around a mailbox and turned onto Forty-fourth at a dead run.

He was breathing hard when he entered his apartment building. He had a split second to decide between the elevator and pounding up seventeen flights of stairs when he noticed the elevator was empty and on the ground floor. He sprinted inside and cursed its slowness as he rode up, realizing he'd left his gun in his bedside drawer.

Fool!

Well, he had his bare hands and hopefully surprise on his side. He'd make the best of them.

Once he reached his floor, he noted that the door wasn't kicked in or damaged in any visible way. He used his key and slipped inside as quietly as he could. He didn't have to search for Sophie; she was right there, bending down at the edge of his living room.

"Sophie," he gasped. "Thank God you're all right."

She rose and turned to face him, looking pale and shaken. "But he is not."

As she turned back to her previous pose, he saw a heaving heap of black-and-brown fur. It took his adrenaline-soaked brain a moment to register that her panic call had nothing to do with the chef who liked to take pot shots at his ex, but with the Doberman.

The dog's flanks quivered, and Vince heard the rasp of labored breathing. He rushed closer and noticed that the dog was shaking all over.

"What happened?" Vince asked, dropping to his knees beside the prostrate animal.

"I don't know. He threw up twice and then . . ." She raised her hands in a helpless gesture. "And then he sort of fell to the ground."

Sophie stared at him in appeal. Standing at the top of the Doberman's head, Mimi gave him the same look. She leaned forward and licked the black trembling head.

"We'd better get him to the vet," Vince decided, thinking the poor old Dob wasn't looking good at all. "Let's go."

He hefted the not inconsiderable bulk of the Doberman in his arms. The dog whimpered a little, but otherwise made no complaint. He carried the dog down and walked the block to where he garaged his SUV, hoping they could make it in time.

Sophie sat in the back, and he laid the dog on the seat beside her, with its head pillowed on her lap. She murmured soothingly and stroked its head.

Fortunately, Vince had lived in this neighborhood long enough that he knew the immediate area intimately. Mimi's fancy vet was in Chelsea, but too far. There was a vet only a few blocks away. He drove like a maniac, heavy on the horn, heavy on the gas, double parked outside the vet's front entrance, and once more lifted his burden.

He wondered if they had a chance of saving the dog. Even in the short time it had taken to travel here, he could see the poor mutt's condition had deteriorated. His eyes rolled in his head, and he was barely breathing.

"Hang on, buddy," he said softly as he hefted the animal into the storefront clinic.

Fortunately, the vet on duty was a young Italian woman who didn't waste any time. Vince walked the dog through to an examining room and laid him on the metal table. Dr. Amanti put the stethoscope to the dog's barely moving chest; she pulled open the eyes, looked into his mouth, and spoke soothingly all the while. The dog vomited once more, a feeble effort at best, then lay back down exhausted.

"What did he last eat?"

"He had a bowl of dog food for breakfast," Vince said. "He hadn't had his dinner yet. Also, he hangs out in the kitchen and eats anything he can find. He got some bread and . . . ah, honey off the floor earlier." He didn't look at Sophie as he said it.

"Did you walk him today?"

"Yes, of course."

"Did he eat any garbage or anything suspicious?"

"No," they said in unison.

"Well, I have to run a couple of tests, but I think he's been poisoned."

"Poisoned? But who would . . . ?"

"How did . . . ?"

"Wait outside now," the vet said. "We'll do what we can for him. I'll let you know."

Sophie held Mimi in her arms, and the dog whined softly as they turned away.

"You're going to be fine," Vince said softly to the Doberman, hoping fiercely he was telling the truth. The stubby tail wagged feebly, and Vince swallowed hard over a sudden lump in his throat.

"Do everything you can," he said to the vet. "Money's no object."

She nodded and smiled, but she didn't look hopeful.

He went out and parked the car, stuffing the ticket he found under the windshield wiper into his pocket, then came back and joined Sophie and Mimi on hard plastic red chairs in the small waiting area. A Siamese cat regarded them balefully, and a parrot in a cage asked *What's up?* in a gravelly parrot voice about a hundred times.

He reached for Sophie's hand, and she held on tight. Mimi lay curled in her lap, whining softly from time to time. They didn't say much, but he had the oddest feeling that they were a family, taking comfort from each other in times of trouble.

Half an hour ticked painfully by, and he tried not to think about what was going on behind the sliding door. An hour, and he was losing hope. Instead of a pesky mutt who ate too much and had invaded his life, the Doberman was to Vince now a loyal guardian who'd done his best to protect Sophie and Mimi. Damn it, the dog was part of his household, and it didn't even have a name.

Well, Sophie's embarrassing girlie name.

Another half hour crawled by. The Siamese had been and gone, the parrot was asking someone somewhere else what was up, and still they sat there.

Suddenly, he couldn't stand it anymore. He went up to the counter and asked the young receptionist, "Can you find out what's going on back there with the Doberman?"

She glanced up, obviously ready to refuse, took one look at his face, and softened. "I can try."

Ten minutes later the vet herself came out, stripping off a pair of latex gloves and looking tired. "Your dog was definitely poisoned. He's stable now, and sleeping. We'll keep him in overnight to keep an eye on him, but I think he's going to make it." She rolled her shoulders as though she'd been bent over for a long time. "The dog's strong and healthy and big enough that he could fight the poison."

She smiled suddenly and pointed to Mimi perched on Sophie's lap. "Be glad it wasn't that one who got to the poison. She wouldn't have had a chance."

She turned away, so she didn't see Vince's expression.

The young receptionist came back out and said, "I'll open a file for your dog. Then you can go home and pick him up in the morning."

"Sure," Vince said, reaching for his wallet.

"Family name?" she asked, tapping on her computer.

"Grange," Vince said, and gave her the address and his phone numbers when she asked.

"Dog's first name?"

The silence was so long, she glanced up from her computer screen. He looked at Sophie and smiled for the first time since he'd received her panic call. "His name's Sir Galahad."

The girl didn't seem to find this a stupid, embarrassing name, merely typed it in. Then asked, "Are his shots up-to-date?"

"I doubt it. We just adopted him. He was a stray."

"When he's back on his feet, you and your wife will want to bring him in for a full physical, and we'll update his shots."

"Sure. Okay," Vince said. Where a few days ago he'd been appalled at the addition of a second dog into his household, now he was happy that he was going to have the chance to come back for yearly physicals and shots.

And she'd called Sophie his wife, and he hadn't said a

word to correct her. In that moment, Vince realized that his life was never going to be the same.

He grinned like a fool.

"What is it?" Sophie asked, seeing him grin.

"They think Sir Galahad's going to be okay."

"Oh, Vince." Tears filled her big blue eyes, and with Mimi tucked under one arm, she rose and threw the other arm around Vince's neck, kissing him with warm, sweet lips that trembled.

"We can pick him up tomorrow."

As Sophie and Mimi headed for the door, he turned back to the receptionist. "Tell the doctor I want to know what kind of poison the dog ingested. I'll want copies of any lab reports and blood work."

"I'll tell her."

"See if she can put a rush on it."

The girl looked startled. "You think someone tried to kill your dog deliberately?"

He shook his head. "I think there was another intended victim."

"Are you suggesting . . . ?"

"Put a rush on those reports. We're talking attempted murder."

Ten

When they got back home, the place seemed half empty without the Doberman. Mimi wandered the apartment, her sharp little nails tapping out her distress on the hardwood.

"She misses him," Sophie said, watching the little dog.

Vince understood. The two dogs had somehow become a matched pair, as unlikely as they seemed together.

A bit like Vince and Sophie. He had a feeling he'd be tracking paths through the hardwood himself if he lost Sophie. The notion had him walking up behind her and pulling her to him for a long, hungry kiss.

She emerged breathless and surprised by his passion—he'd surprised himself. How had she become important to him so fast?

"I made a mistake, Sophie. A stupid-ass obvious mistake."

She blinked. "You did?"

He nodded, kissed her again quickly because he couldn't help himself. "I don't think you were ever in danger." He crouched low and tapped his knee. Mimi stopped her aimless wandering and raced toward him, ears flying, pink nails sparkling. He scooped her up and held her to his chest where she showed her affection by licking his chin. "Mimi was the target. You and the Doberman got in the way."

Sophie blinked, and gave him the same look his mother used to right before she'd put her hand on his forehead to test for fever. "Mimi?"

"Yeah. You know how I said I'd inherited her?"

"Of course."

"Well, she was also a beneficiary of my aunt's will. To the tune of fourteen million bucks."

Sophie's eyes widened, and she glanced at Mimi as though she couldn't believe anything so little could be so rich. "Mimi inherited . . . ?"

"Yeah. I inherited Mimi, and I'll get her money when she passes on. But there was one stipulation. If Mimi dies of unnatural causes—that is, if she gets offed—the money goes to my cousins instead. My aunt was probably trying to prevent me from snuffing her to get the money, but what she didn't think of was that my charming cousins might do the job. I can't believe I didn't think of it earlier. I was too busy thinking of you."

"You have cousins who would murder a sweet little dog?"

"I wouldn't have thought I did, but it's the only explanation. Think about it. The Doberman didn't eat anything but dog food until I threw him those cookies. Right after he ate them he got sick—I bet the cookies were poisoned. And the vet said Mimi would have died if she'd eaten them instead. It was his size that saved Sir Galahad."

"But . . . where did the biscuits come from?"

"They were packed with a bunch of Mimi's stuff that came when she moved in here. Every time I tried to give her one, she turned up her nose, so I shoved them in the cupboard. Why would my aunt stock cookies the dog doesn't like? Doesn't make sense."

Sophie rubbed the heel of her hand against her forehead. "So, you say your cousins planted a tin of poison biscuits and also tried to have the dog kidnapped and then shot? It seems a little . . . *incroyable.*"

"Yeah, I know." He started to pace, Mimi bobbing along

in his arms. "But think about it. The first day you were out, we thought you were being mugged because of her collar. Maybe it wasn't the collar they were after, but the dog."

"I suppose it's possible," she agreed, flopping to a chair and watching him.

"When you got shot at the next day, you were holding Mimi in your arms, weren't you?"

Sophie's eyes narrowed. "I'm not sure. Let me think." She nodded. "Yes, yes, I was. She grew tired, poor little thing, so I carried her the last part of the way. But how do you . . ." She gasped and touched her arm. "Oh, I see."

He nodded. "They shot at the dog while she was in your arms. And missed. If the dog had been walking, you'd have a scab on your ankle. Or Mimi would be dead."

"How could anyone do such a thing?"

"They're not the brightest pair." He sat beside Sophie on the couch, and the dog curled in his lap. "You said you never saw the supposed mugger?"

"No. It was a man, and he had a woolen cap pulled low on his head. Sir Galahad took a chunk of his blue jeans, though. I saved it."

"Good. I'm betting Jonathon and Esme are trying to do this themselves. They wouldn't want to hire anyone to do their dirty work since that would make them vulnerable to blackmail. Which is lucky for us. Let's face it, a pro would have done a better job."

"I am lucky to have been wounded by an amateur," Sophie said with some bitterness.

He grinned at her. "A pro wouldn't have tried to shoot the dog while you were holding it. You'd have come out of this uninjured, but I doubt Mimi would still be with us."

"Ah, well, then." The lift of her shoulders was as French as her perfume.

"I'm going to make certain my precious cousins are stopped in their tracks." He patted Mimi's curly head so she sighed in her sleep. She might be an embarrassment to the name dog, but she was his, and he'd developed a grudging affection for her.

"But how will you stop them?" Sophie asked.

He let out a breath. "We'll have to lay a trap."

"But surely this Esme and Jonathon will suspect a trap?" Sophie felt nervous and flustered. She was good with children and animals. She was a marvelous cook. But an entrapper of criminals? *Mais, non.*

"Relax," Vince said, looking as though he was having far too much fun for her peace of mind. "We'll do great."

"I don't think Sir Galahad is well enough yet for visitors," she said hopefully, though in truth the dog had recovered remarkably in the two days he'd been home.

"Forget it. He wants a piece of them, don't you, boy?" Vince said, rubbing the dog's head so he rolled to his back and waved all four paws in the air in obvious invitation. With a low chuckle, Vince squatted and rubbed the dog's belly. If there could be anything good to come out of a dog poisoning, it was that Vince had come to appreciate Sir Galahad. He called him by his name now and had clearly come to realize the dog belonged in his household.

Vince was so big and gruff, but she wondered if he even realized what a soft heart he hid under all his tough-guy bluster. He was sweet with the dogs, by turns tender and raunchy with her. She shook herself as she caught herself smiling like a simpleton while Mimi trotted over to share in Sir Galahad's attention. When big, tough Vince picked Mimi up and laid her over his shoulder, where she draped herself like a fluffy white stole, Sophie fell in love with the man.

No, she thought as the realization pumped through her, she hadn't fallen in love that second, she'd only just let herself accept her feelings.

Love. And with another American! As she waited for the panic and horror of her situation to sink in her stomach like an emotional *Titanic,* her feelings continued buoyant. In fact, she couldn't keep the smile off her face. Apart from their nationality, Vince and Gregory didn't have a thing in common. This time, her heart had chosen well.

And if the man she loved wanted to play detective in order to protect the dogs he'd grown fond of, then she supposed she was going to have to pull herself together and help him.

"All right," she said. "What is the plan?"

"We invite them for lunch."

Her eyes widened so suddenly she felt her eyelashes scrape her lids. "Am I supposed to poison them?"

Vince laughed. "Tempting. But I have something else in mind. I've got a few calls to make to set things up."

"Phoh," she said, when Vince returned from taking Sir Galahad across the hall to 17B. He'd hired the neighbor's boy to look after the dog for a few hours while the sting operation went down in 17A.

She ran her hands down the front of her short black skirt on her way to check on the lunch. The food at least would be good. Everything else made her nervous.

"Why did you have to invite them for lunch?" she asked as she stirred soup. "I hate these people."

"Stop fidgeting. You'll do fine." He hoisted Mimi to his shoulder, where she perched like a fluffy angel.

"I wish I could hide next door."

"I need you here. My partner in crime busting," he said and kissed her swiftly. Then he raised his head and with one hand touched her cheek. "My partner in—"

The doorbell chimed, so she jumped with nerves, and Vince stopped in midsentence to kiss her once again. Hard and swift. "Here's something to take your mind off the charade," he said, his eyes crinkling as he stared into her eyes the way he did sometimes when he was deep inside her body and moving toward climax. "I love you."

While her mouth opened and closed a couple of times, he grinned at her once more and kissed her open mouth. Then he went for the door.

It was all right for him, addling her brains and making love to her mouth, then telling her he loved her. All right for him to tell her to relax; she had the pivotal role in this farce.

He loved her.

Oh, she wished he'd chosen a better time for his declaration. Given her time to assure him in the most obvious way that she returned his sentiments.

She glanced at a million dollars an ounce Mimi, yapping from Vince's shoulder, thought of Sir Galahad next door, who was still moving slowly.

She watched Vince's strong, broad back as he opened the door. The man she loved. The man who loved her. She wouldn't let them down. She wouldn't let any of them down.

She was smiling and calm when Vince ushered in two similar-looking, expensively dressed and groomed cousins. Jonathon did his best to look down her shirt when he was introduced and held her hand a little too long. Esme didn't stoop to shake hands with the staff, merely nodded, gazing at her with cold eyes.

So the woman was a snob and her brother a lech. Just a couple more counts to add to their rap sheet along with attempted murder.

Vince poured them all a glass of dry white wine, and Sophie brought out a tray of hors d'oeuvres, and they sat sipping and munching for a few awkward minutes.

"Really, Vince, I can't believe you're still in this dismal apartment now you're a multimillionaire," Esme said by way of an opening conversational gambit.

"Not me," he replied with a smile. "Mimi's the multimillionaire."

She laughed. "You'll hardly let an insane old woman's will stop you from spending a fortune."

"We'll see," he replied noncommittally, but Sophie saw the

flare of anger in his eyes. He didn't talk about Aunt Marjorie much, but she could tell he'd been fond of the woman.

"As flattered as we are to be invited for a family reunion," Jonathon drawled, "what's up?"

"It's Mimi." The dog, who'd jumped on Sophie's lap the minute she sat down, raised her head when she heard her name. "I was wondering if you'd take her while Sophie and I go away for a few days."

Esme put her glass down with a decided snap. "You're sleeping with the housekeeper? Oh, Vince."

"*Salope,*" Sophie whispered into Mimi's ear, and she could have sworn Mimi nodded agreement. Before Vince called his cousin something worse in her own language, which she could see he was about to do, Sophie spoke up. "I'm not the house-keeper. I'm Mimi's nanny."

The superior smirk the woman sent her had her gritting her teeth. "Sure you are."

She rose, knowing they had to get this horror show moving. It was no longer herself she was worried about blowing the operation, but Vince. He looked as if he wanted to toss both of his cousins out. And from the look on his face, he'd send them through the seventeenth-floor window.

While Vince and his cousins worked out arrangements for the supposed dog-sitting assignment, she played her part in the kitchen. "Vince," she called out. "What have you done with my tarragon?"

"Is that a spice?"

"*Bien sûr.*"

"I put it on the top shelf in the cupboard beside the oven. It's not like you ever need them."

"I do," she snapped. "I like flavor in my food." She drag-ged a kitchen chair to the cupboard in question and climbed onto it, revealing the maximum leg possible knowing that Jonathon, at least, would be watching. She retrieved the spice and then reached behind it. "Oh," she said. "What's this, Vince?"

"Hmm? Don't know. Never seen it." He was lying because he'd fed the poor Doberman from the tin she was now holding not three days ago.

She eased open the lid, careful not to look into the living area. "Imbecile," she said. "It is cookies. Dog cookies."

"Oh, probably from that stuff of Mimi's. There was so much of that junk I put it away and probably forgot about it."

She clambered down and placed the tin on the counter, then added the tarragon to her Minestrone de Coques et Saint-Jaques.

They managed to get through the lunch with more cordiality, and she couldn't help but notice her "discovery" had caused Esme and Jonathon to drop the hostility. While they professed themselves delighted to dog sit Mimi for a few days, Sophie noticed how often Jonathon's eyes strayed to the kitchen counter where she'd so casually left the tin with the cute hand-painted poodle design.

Vince had assured her his cousins wouldn't put off their murderous intent until they were dog sitting Mimi because, if she died mysteriously under their care, it would be too obvious they'd killed her.

A private investigator friend of Vince's had arranged for the original biscuits to be tested, and they were, as Vince had suspected, laced with poison. The same poison that nearly killed Sir Galahad. But there was no proof that Esme and Jonathon were to blame. At least, not yet.

She only hoped the trap they were setting caught the two thoroughly unlikable cousins.

After they'd finished eating, Sophie said, "I'll put coffee on." She was a little nervous now, since the next part of their plan involved getting themselves out of the main rooms without causing suspicion. It was the weakest part of their strategy as well as the most important.

She was about to deliver her oft-rehearsed line about running down to the corner store to get the coffee she'd supposedly run out of. When she reached the main entrance she'd have the doorman buzz Vince and tell him to come down and bring her some money. She had to play a spoilt princess and refuse to come back up. Neither of them liked the idea of leaving Mimi alone in the apartment with the cousins, though.

She took time to arrange cups and fiddle with cream and sugar, putting off the moment she'd pretend there was no coffee, when she caught a look that passed between Jonathon and Esme and decided to wait a minute.

Her patience was soon rewarded.

"Sophie," Esme said, rising from her chair. "Can I speak to you privately about something?"

The woman had been condescending to downright rude, and now she wanted to speak in private? Vince was right. These two weren't all that bright. Thank goodness. "But of course."

"Excuse us," Esme said, and walked to Vince's bedroom. Sophie didn't dare look at Vince as she followed in his cousin's wake.

Once they got into the bedroom, Esme shut the door and said, "Um, look. I'm sorry if I was a little hostile earlier. It's just that I care about Vince. He's been hurt by women before."

If Vince had been hurt by women, he carried no scars, and he certainly hadn't told Sophie about it. "Oh, that's sad," she said.

Esme sank down onto his bed, crossed her long, elegant legs, and gazed at Sophie. "I don't want to see him hurt again."

"Are you asking me what are my intentions?" she asked, trying very hard not to laugh.

"Well. Um. Yes. Yes, that's exactly it. I am."

"Okay, well, I can tell you—"

"Wait!" the other woman stuck a hand in the air as though she were about to summon a head waiter. "I don't want to do this behind Vince's back. I think we should be completely open." And without giving Sophie a chance to say a thing, she called out, "Vince, honey, Sophie and I would like to see you in the bedroom."

The soft male rumble of voices ceased from outside the door, and Vince said, "Okay," as though it were perfectly normal for women to tag team him in his bedroom. Hmm.

He arrived in a moment and shut the door behind him. He shot Sophie a brief glance so full of meaning she had to turn her head.

"Now, Vince, I asked you to come in because Sophie is about to tell me what her intentions are toward you."

His devilish eyes glittered with amusement, and something more. Something that made Sophie's heart forget to beat.

"Well, good," he said, climbing onto the bed beside where Esme perched and crawling up to the headboard. He stacked a couple of pillows behind him and settled back, long legs crossed at the ankle. "As a matter of fact, Esme. I'd like to know her intentions, too."

Torn between wanting to laugh and wanting to strangle him for putting her into this absurd position, she decided if he wanted to play silly, daring games, she could play, too.

"My intentions are perfectly honorable," she said.

He rubbed his jaw with one hand. "Define honorable. Would we be talking marriage here?"

Her nostrils flared slightly, and she stared across Esme at her lover, who was settled comfortably as though he planned to stay there awhile. "But of course. I want my six children to be legitimate."

She had the satisfaction of seeing his eyes widen for a second, but it was Esme who squeaked, "Six kids?"

"I like children. I'm very good with them," she explained, then smiled a smile so warm it would melt chocolate. "You don't mind, do you, darling?"

"Well, honey, I was kind of thinking two kids myself."

"Bah. Two *petits enfants*? It's not enough."

"Now, Esme," he said, turning to the woman who was sitting on the bed with a stupefied expression on her face. "I'm going to ask you to help us here. Kind of like a mediator. This is the work I usually do, but obviously, since I'm an involved party, I can't do the mediating. I think I see a middle ground here. Sophie wants six kids, I was thinking of two. A good negotiator will find a compromise that both parties can live with."

Esme stood and stared from Vince to Sophie and back again. "Are you suggesting you split the difference and have four kids?"

"Damn, you're good," Vince said, approval in his tone. "You'd make a terrific negotiator if you ever decide you'd like to work."

"I can't believe you'd consider four kids. Do you have any idea how much mess and noise they create?"

He smiled at Sophie, and she felt the warm caress of his tilted lips almost as though he were kissing her. "I'm looking forward to them."

Somehow this whole thing was feeling less jokey and absurd than when she'd thrown down the six-fingered gauntlet a moment ago. Instead of making him faint with panic, she felt a little that way herself. She'd intended to back him into a corner, so why did she feel intersecting walls nudging her spine?

Her eyes narrowed. She wasn't nearly done. "Naturally, they will all be educated in France. My children must grow up French."

"We'll spend summers in France, so they'll be comfortable in both cultures."

"But, but," she spluttered, appalled at how utterly appealing this ridiculous scenario felt, "you can't even speak the language."

"I'll learn," he said. "You'll teach me. You and Mimi."

"Mimi," she gasped. For those crazy minutes she'd allowed herself to imagine a future with Vince and her and children, she'd forgotten they were acting out this charade because of Mimi.

The sound of the dog's name seemed to act on Esme, too. She said, "I want you two to stay right here and talk to each other for a few minutes. We'll wait." She smiled like a shark scenting blood. "Jonathon and I will be right outside. I can't wait to tell him the good news that you're finally settling down, Vince." And she hustled out of the room, shutting the door with a click behind her.

"Do you think we've given them enough time?" Sophie asked, her eyes fixed nervously on Vince, who was off the bed and advancing on her.

"Let's give them a little more." And he pulled her hard against him and kissed her.

She kissed him back. Well, what else was she going to do when his big body surrounded her, pulled her in, and held her close?

"I am completely crazy about you," he informed her in a husky tone, staring down into her face as though he wanted to imprint this moment forever.

She tried to chuckle, but it came out more like a heartfelt sigh. "Me and my six children."

He kissed her again. Quick and sweet. "Four. And I meant every word. Let's go."

Since she was currently speechless, she let him pull her by the hand and escort her back into the other room.

Jonathon was holding Esme's leather coat while she slipped her arms into the sleeves.

He smiled the identical shark-looking-forward-to-feeding-time smile as his sister. "So, I guess you're engaged now. Congratulations. We're going to give you two some privacy. We'll call you."

Mimi was sitting in the kitchen, her little pink tongue licking crumbs off the floor, but tore herself away to trot to the door with everyone else. After they'd bid the cousins farewell, and handshakes and kisses had been exchanged, they shut the door and turned to each other.

"Do you think they bought it?" he whispered.

Still unable to speak, she nodded.

"Let's see."

He walked to where the video recorder was sitting discreetly on a shelf where he'd set it up earlier.

He rewound the tape and watched it in the viewing screen. Sophie came close, and by putting their heads side by side they could both watch. He fast-forwarded until a mini Esme and a mini Sophie left the room. Then he slowed the film to normal and watched as a tiny version of himself left. He put an arm around Sophie, feeling her tension as well as his own.

"Yes!" he cried softly as he watched on film as Jonathon glanced around, then went straight to the cookie tin.

Mimi came running when she saw the bone-shaped treats, and they watched her eat one and then take a second one from Jonathon.

"That was a great idea of yours to rub those cookies with foie gras," he conceded, watching the finicky Mimi polish off the second cookie.

"Yes. Even the fresh batch from the gourmet dog treat place didn't thrill her."

She leaned her head on Vince's shoulder when he'd stopped the film and put the recorder down.

"I didn't like them, but I can't believe those two would try to harm such a sweet dog."

He snorted. "Those two would sell their mother and father's organs if the price was high enough."

"Is this film enough to stop them?"

"It's pretty good. The rats have taken the cheese, but they haven't fully sprung the trap yet."

"What now?"

"I'm going to bring Sir Galahad home, and when I get back, you'd better be naked."

Eleven

At noon the next day, Vince called his cousin Jonathon. "Hey, thanks for offering to dog sit, but we've changed our minds. We're not going away after all."

"Why not?" Jonathon asked, the fake concern not remotely masking his glee.

"It's just that . . . uh, we decided with the wedding and all that we've got too much to do to take a vacation."

"I understand. If you change your mind . . ."

"Oh, we won't."

"No problem. Hey, after yesterday, Esme was saying how much she misses seeing Mimi. How about we come and take her for a walk?"

"Take Mimi for a walk?" Vince tried to inject the right mixture of panic and bravado into his tone. "Thanks. But we already took her for a long one. She's pretty burned out. Maybe some other time."

"Did they believe you?" Sophie asked when he ended the call.

"Oh, no." He chuckled. "They think Mimi's breathed her last."

At six o'clock the police arrived. With the male officer were Esme and Jonathon and the family lawyer.

Vince blinked at the entourage. Before he finished asking what was going on, Jonathon said, "We want to see Mimi."

"She's not here."

Esme burst into noisy tears and said, "You killed her, I know you did."

Vince scratched his head and said, "Maybe you'd all better come inside."

Esme marched in and called, "Mimi? Mimi?" in a heart-rending voice that would have got Meryl Streep nominated for another Oscar and proceeded to throw open both the bedroom doors.

"Where is she? I know you killed her. You never liked her. We're going to press charges, order an autopsy."

"And don't forget the part where you overthrow Great-aunt Marjorie's will," Vince said pleasantly.

Jonathon sent him a glance of intense dislike. "Go ahead and joke about it, but you can't produce the dog, can you?"

"Would someone please explain what is going on?" the lawyer asked sharply.

"Mimi's dead." Esme sobbed louder. "Vince killed her."

"What makes you accuse him of this crime?" the lawyer asked, pinching the knife pleats of his dress trousers and raising the pant leg slightly before sitting down in Vince's favorite chair.

As though he'd told them to, Jonathon and Esme also sat, on the couch facing him. Vince pulled a pine kitchen chair over and completed the family group.

The cop positioned himself between them and the door but remained standing.

"We came yesterday to visit Mimi. I had a premonition," Esme explained, raising tear-filled periwinkle eyes to the lawyer and tossing the long curtain of black hair over her shoulder.

She shook her head as though she couldn't bear to go on.

"Mimi didn't look well," Jonathon said, patting his sister on the knee and picking up where she'd presumably left off.

"She seemed sick. Vince insisted she was fine, but he looked guilty. We offered to take Mimi for a few days."

"That's not true," Vince exclaimed, because he thought the cousins would expect something from him, and he didn't want them suspicious quite yet.

Once again Esme got herself under control enough to raise a shaking finger and point it at Vince. "And this morning he called to cancel Mimi's visit. He wouldn't even let us come and take her for a walk. She's dead, I know it. Vince murdered Mimi."

Vince picked up his phone and punched out a number. "You can come home now," he said when Sophie answered. Since she was only at the neighbors' it didn't take her more than a minute to show up with both dogs in tow.

The Doberman's stump tail began to wag when he saw Vince, as though he'd been stuck with French women far too long.

Mimi took one look at all the people gathered and began to bark excitedly.

As Sir Galahad came toward Vince he suddenly stopped and stiffened, going from big sucky lap dog to ferocious guard dog in a second. His neck fur stood on end, and his lips pulled back in a snarl. In the tiny pauses between Mimi's hysterical yapping, the ominous sound of his growl could be heard.

Sir Galahad wasn't looking at Vince anymore; he was looking at Jonathon.

"Oh, what a clever doggie you are," Sophie said. "You remember this one, *hein?* He's the one who tried to take Mimi my first day on the job, and you were so brave, you came and saved us."

Jonathon was inching closer to Esme, who was herself scuttling as far from the growling Doberman as she could get. "What is that beast doing in here? Get him out!"

Unimpressed by any of the antics, the lawyer only had eyes for the clearly healthy poodle who, competing for atten-

tion with the Doberman, was doing her best to grab the lime-
light by twirling on her hind legs in the center of the assembled group, accompanying herself with high-pitched barks.

"Mimi appears quite healthy to me," said the lawyer in a
tone loud enough to be heard above the racket.

"But that can't be Mimi!" Esme cried, trying to hide behind Jonathon at the same time he was trying to hide behind
her.

Plan B was being screwed up as thoroughly as Plan A had
been yesterday, but, Vince suspected, with similarly success-
ful results. Deciding he liked watching Jonathon and Esme
suffer for their crimes, he didn't call off Sir Galahad.

Besides, Sophie's temper was simmering, and she looked
like a combination sex goddess and avenging angel standing
there, so he decided to let her take this scene wherever it led
her and settled back to enjoy himself.

"Of course it's Mimi," Sophie cried. "No thanks to you.
Yes, that's right, Sir Galahad. Hold them there. Good dog."

And she ran into the princess bedroom only to return with
a torn piece of badly tooth-marked denim. Oh, damn it, she
was good, his Sophie. Holding the piece of denim aloft, she
said to Jonathon, "Do you recognize this?"

She glanced from the lawyer to the cop, who seemed to be
enjoying the drama as much as Vince himself was.

Jonathon yelled, "Get this dog off me. Somebody do
something."

"He recognizes your scent," Sophie said in a tone that
could only be called smug. "If I gave him this piece of your
jeans—they are yours, aren't they? You were wearing them
when you assaulted us—and told him to attack, I wonder
what he'd do . . ." She cast a glance at Vince from under her
lashes, and he nearly laughed aloud. God, he loved this
woman.

"Don't you dare. I'll sue you if that bastard bites me."

"Or me," Esme put in.

"What do you think, Vince?" Sophie asked.

"I think Sir Galahad could do some serious damage to Jonathon if that hunk of blue jeans has his scent on it."

Slowly, she lowered the torn fabric. The Doberman was pacing in front of the couch, still growling low in his throat, hackles up in warning. He made it clear to all that he was only waiting for the word and he'd sink the very sharp teeth he'd bared into Jonathon.

The temptation to let the dog at his murderous cousin was almost irresistible.

Sweat dampened Jonathon's pale brow as she brought the cloth closer to the big dog. "I know he will attack if I tell him to, but, Vince, do we know for sure he can be called off?"

"Never tried it," Vince answered truthfully.

Sir Galahad had caught the scent of the denim, and his growls became louder. Frankly, Vince wasn't sure how well trained he was anyway. They were playing with fire here. Just as he was about to call a halt, Jonathon shouted, "All right. It was me. Now get that fucking dog out of here."

"Here, Sir Galahad." Vince called him, and after giving one very low, *don't think this is over* growl, the Doberman stalked to Vince's side and sat, still tense and alert.

"Good boy."

"I really think someone had best explain what this is all about," said the lawyer once again.

"I'm going to tell you a little story," Vince said. "And then we'll watch a movie. What you'll understand by the end of it is that my precious cousins here have been trying to murder Mimi to get their hands on Aunt Marjorie's fourteen million bucks."

"That's ridiculous," Esme snapped, her tears forgotten.

But, by the time he and Sophie had told their story, and everyone present had watched the video recording of Esme getting the two of them out of the room while Jonathon fed Mimi the cookies he'd believed were poisoned, his claims didn't seem ridiculous. After he'd provided copies of the toxicology report on the original cookies from the original tin, and the lab reports on the Doberman, the cousins had pretty much shut up and glared sullenly at the floor.

He gave copies of everything to the lawyer, who said, "Jonathon and Esme, if it were in my power to revoke the money your great-aunt left you, I'd do it. Sadly it isn't, but I can promise that no matter what happens to Mimi, you two will never get another cent from your aunt's estate." Then he rose, patted Mimi perfunctorily on the head, shook Vince's hand, nodded to Sophie and the police officer, then left.

There was a moment of uncomfortable silence. "Ma'am," said the cop. "Do you want to press charges against these two? They shot at you."

She looked at Jonathon and Esme, at Mimi and Sir Galahad, and finally at Vince. "No," she said softly. "I don't."

"I'm opening a case file on this anyway," his buddy, Ed the cop, said, staring down at the cousins. "I find out you two are so much as jaywalking and your asses are mine. Got it?"

Miserable nods. "You'd better go before they change their minds."

Without another word, and only a backward glance at the Doberman, they scuttled out the door. Sir Galahad, denied his pound of flesh, gave a bark/snarl combo that speeded them on their way.

"Thanks for doing this, Ed," Vince said, shaking his old friend's hand.

"Anytime, Bulldog. After you warned me they'd probably go to the cops, I made sure their call got routed to me." He chuckled suddenly. "I don't think they'll be bothering you again."

After he left, Vince found Sophie on the floor, hugging both dogs to her. What the hell, he thought as he joined them there.

"You know," he said as the Doberman knocked into one of the tables, and Mimi leaped out of the way catching her paw in a lamp cord, "we're going to have to get a bigger place."

"I beg your pardon?"

Vince grinned at her, this woman he'd been waiting for all his life. "Two of us, two dogs, and four kids on the way." He looked around his two-bedroom apartment. "We're going to need a bigger place."

"Oh, but, Vince," she said, her voice catching and her eyes shining. "I didn't mean—"

"I did." He kissed her. Then Mimi kissed her. Then Sir Galahad slobbered all over them both. And they were laughing, and hugging, and he knew that nothing was ever going to be the same again.

"I love you," he said.

"I love you, too." She laughed and threw herself at him. "And you'll really learn French?"

"I have a feeling that's going to be the easy part . . . Come on," he said, hauling her to her feet.

"Where are you taking me?"

"To bed."

At the door to his room he stopped and turned to confront two canines eager to continue the game they'd started on the floor. "And you two are not invited."

With a tiny yap of disappointment, his fourteen million dollar poodle minced off to leap onto his favorite chair. The Doberman made a grumbling sound and followed Mimi, bypassing the chair to take the couch.

"Are we really going to have four children?" Sophie asked once they were alone.

He slipped his hand under her sweater and palmed her breasts just the way she liked.

"Honey," he said, "everything's negotiable."

THE WORLD
IS TOO
DARNED BIG

MaryJanice
Davidson

For everyone who wanted to be the star of their own movie.

Acknowledgments

Writing a novel is a lot like running a marathon. But the novella is more like a forty-yard dash: you've got to get your ass in gear right away. I love this shorter length and am grateful to Alex Kendall, of Red Sage Publishing, for being the first to give me the chance to show readers that I could dash reasonably well. And to Kate Duffy, of Brava, for letting me run wherever I want.

Prologue

"You know, bad guys trying to blow my head off isn't as much fun as I thought it would be," Benjamin commented. "It's more stressful than anything else."

"Typical," Tara said. "Felony assault—it's all hype."

"Any bright ideas on how to get out of this?"

"Ben, I am *so* not the brains of this team. Besides, it's your fault we're even here."

"The hell! You're the one who wanted to steal the world."

"I didn't want to steal the *world*, just a few key pieces of it, not that it's any of your business. *You're* the one who insisted we save humanity." Tara invested the phrase with heavy sarcasm. "Could there be a bigger waste of time? No? Ask the guy with the gun if you don't believe me."

"Fine. Anyway, we'd better get out of here before bullets start exploring our temporal lobes. This hallway isn't going to provide cover much longer."

"So? Think of something, gadget man." Tara stretched out her long, long legs and closed her eyes. "Let me know what you come up with."

He watched, dumbfounded, as she went to sleep. She could always do that. It was unbelievably aggravating.

He leaned over and shouted into her gorgeous, still face,

"And I did *not* get us into this!" In the distance, the firing pop of the silencer accentuated his statement.

"Did, too," Tara said without opening her eyes.

"Did not!"

"Don't you remember?"

As a matter of fact, he did.

One

Earlier that day . . .

Bored, Benjamin Dyson put the finishing touches on his Universal remote—a *true* Universal remote, thank you very much—one that would work on any television set in the world, provided it had been built since 1992 . . . which was to say, 92.56% of them.

It also doubled as a cell phone.

Well, super. Another gadget, completed well before deadline. The rep from the CIA would be here any minute—or was this one for Honeywell? The Secret Service? It was getting hard to keep them all straight. He could look it up in the log, but frankly, didn't care enough. If he wasn't going to get to use the gadget *du jour* in the field, he didn't much care who did.

He yawned and scribbled an invoice, picking a number out of the air—seventeen hundred? Thirty-three hundred? What did he care? He had more money than he'd ever be able to spend. Not that the government was exactly known for paying Net 30. Or even Net 150. Well, it was his patriotic duty. He supposed.

He heard the car pull in and hit the garage door button

clipped to his desk. The sun had come up just an hour or so ago, and the fresh-faced agent in the *de rigueur* unmarked sedan looked entirely too perky for this time of the day as he popped out of his car and practically trotted into the garage.

"Hey, Dr. Dyson! How you doing today?"

"Fine, Tom." Bored, Ben started to hand over the remote and the paperwork. After a moment's thought, he stuffed it all into a used grocery bag from Piggly Wiggly.

"Thanks for the phone call. My supervisor couldn't believe it. A week ahead of schedule!" Agent Tom Carradine shook his head admiringly. "Unreal! You're worth all of our lab weenies put together."

"Is that what I am?" he asked, amused. "A lab weenie?"

"Uh, no offense, Ben. Without you guys, we wouldn't last very long out in The World, you know?"

"Yeah, yeah." Ben yawned again.

"And I must say," Tom said, looking around, "this is the most sterile garage I have ever been in. You could eat off the floor in here."

"Thanks for the visual. Listen, see if you can get Accounts Payable to cough it up a little sooner this time, willya?"

"Not my department," Tom said with irritating cheer. He smoothed back his shiny black hair—Tom needed to lay off the styling products—and clicked the remote at Ben in a friendly way. Behind him, inside the house, Ben could hear his television turning on. "Thanks again. Catch you later."

"Buh," he grunted, taking a swallow of his hot chocolate. He could see Tom was washing his hands of the whole Accounts Payable situation—the typical action of anyone *not* in Accounts Payable—but was too filled with ennui to stop the process.

Tom trotted back to his sedan, and Ben watched him go, then hit the garage door switch until the street slid from sight.

Now what? Take a month off? The Cape was nice this time of year. He supposed he could think about Thanks-

giving . . . His parents were still touring the state park system
in their RV, but his sister and her new husband would be glad
to have him over for dinner. That sounded nice and homey
and traditional and . . .

He yawned again.

For the millionth time, he thought about applying at one
of the academies, or giving his guy at Langley a call. Sure! He
could go through the training patch and be in the field by
springtime . . . summer at the latest. He could . . . could . . .

Get his head blown off. He was thirty-four . . . not exactly
prime recruiting age for field agents. He had played it safe
and stayed in the lab, and made himself indispensable, and
rich. Now it was too late for adventures.

*There is plenty of adventure to be had on the other end of
a microscope,* his physics teacher had been fond of saying.
His physics teacher had been as round as he was tall and felt
the worst thing to happen to an invention was to have people
use it. Dr. Thorson was all theory. Had a heart attack in his
very own lab, as a matter of fact. One supposed you could
say he died with his boots on. Died with his slide rule in his
pocket? Was that even—

For God's sake, he grumbled, dumping another packet of
Swiss Miss into his mug. *Stop complaining, you morbid
fuck! You've got a great life. A great, safe life. You get paid to
tinker, to think shit up.*

Right.

Damn right.

"Oh, fuck," he said, and rested his head on his forearms.

Two

How could he have let this happen? How could he become a supporting actor in someone else's movie? He'd always fantasized about being Bond, but the plain truth was, he wasn't Bond and never had been and never would be, and that was that, amen and forever. He was Q. He was . . . What had Tom called him? A lab weenie?

He heard a car pull up, one with a powerful engine under the hood—cripes, had they strapped a wild animal in there?—and shrugged. Secret service? No, they didn't like the flashy cars. Private dick? No, they couldn't afford the flashy cars. Local law enforcement? No, they couldn't catch the flashy cars. Field agent? Maybe. Whoever it was, *he* was officially on vacation.

As if in response to the garage door not going up, the car's engine roared, sounding exactly like a pissed-off Bengal in heat. Ben clapped his hands over his ears, then decided it would be easier to tell double-oh fuckhead face-to-face that he was on vacation. He hit the button to raise the door.

The engine cut off abruptly, and a door slammed shut. Then he saw a pair of shoes walk around and wait by the door.

The left shoe—a red sneaker with black laces and a black

skull and crossbones inked on the toe—started tapping impatiently as the door continued to rise, revealing black leggings, a hip-skimming cherry red baby tee—and what hips!—firm-looking, perfectly rounded breasts, a swanlike neck, sharp chin, Angelina Jolie lips (colored to match her T-shirt), tip-tilted nose (pierced with a tiny silver skull), greenish gray eyes, and close-cropped white-blond hair.

"Whoa," was the best he could do.

"Dr. Dyson," the vision said. She was tall—her head passed a bare six inches from the top of his garage door as she entered. "Make me wait a *little* longer next time."

"Okay. Nice mouse."

"Thank you." She stroked the rat, which was as long as her forearm and as white as freshly fallen snow. "It's a Norway Black."

"But it's white."

"Yes."

"Okay." He tried to stop staring at her. The rat didn't help. She was larger than life, and that voice! So husky and low, the woman made Kathleen Turner sound as though she was breathing helium. "What can I do for you?" *Please, please let it be something involving nudity and raspberries . . .*

"I need you to make something for me."

"Oh, I can't."

She arched blond brows. The rat sneered in his general direction. "*You* can't? That'll be a first. You're sort of famous, you know, in certain circles."

Now *there* was a nerve-wracking idea. "I mean, I'm on vacation."

"You're hanging out in your garage on vacation? Although, I have to say, this is the nicest, cleanest garage I've ever—"

"It's my lab," he snapped. "And yes."

"Terrific," she said, and stroked the rat some more, looking around. She strolled over to a wall of cell phones and almost touched one, then seemed to think better of it.

He was weirdly reminded of a Bond villain, and half expected her to say something like, "More tea, Mr. Bond? Mwah-hah-hah!"

"So, thanks for stopping by and all, but, see, I'm on vacation now, and—"

"I guess I could stick my gun in your ear and ask again," she mused.

"I don't think the CIA would like that."

"CIA?"

"Well, maybe Honeywell. Halliburton. Hell's Angels. Somebody wouldn't like it. I'm almost positive. And I don't work for the bad guys. Although, if I was going to break that rule, I sure would in your case. You're six feet tall, right?"

"Six-one," she said absently. "Dr. Dyson, you dope, you *already* work for the bad guys. Who did you think wanted the skeleton key card?"

"The CIA."

She raised her eyebrows at him again.

"Oh, fuck," he said. "But they had all the IDs. And the PO. It was even signed by their head buyer!"

"Oh, so they weren't *sloppy* bad guys."

"God dammit," he cursed.

"Anyway, I want one, too."

"One what?"

"I thought you were some kind of genius."

"Some kind of idiot is more like it," he muttered, and she laughed. It seemed to startle the rat, who froze in her arms. "Of course, this is assuming you're telling the truth about the good guys really being bad guys."

"Why would I lie about that?" she asked reasonably. "What do I get out of it?"

"How the hell should I know? And FYI, this is the most surreal conversation I've had this week."

"Yeah, well, it's not really working for me, either. Look, don't beat yourself up. I mean it—put that board down," she ordered. "With all the stuff you crank out, you were bound to trip up eventually."

"They fooled me. They *fooled* me. *Me.*" He remembered the card well; an actual challenge, for a change, and good money, which he expected. The go-between had shown up about twenty minutes before Agent Tom. And he'd never suspected a thing.

"Take it easy," she said. "So, I take it you're not going to—"

"Dammit!"

"Well, crud. If you're not going to make me one, and if I'm not going to *make* you make me one, I guess I'll go steal it from the bad guys, then. See ya."

"Wait!" He was frantically digging through his desk, the file cabinets, the hidden compartment in the back of his mini-fridge. He grabbed a blackberry yogurt, peeked at the label, and stuffed it into his satchel. "I'm coming with you," he said over his shoulder. "They can get into any building in the world with that card."

"I thought you were on vacation."

"Well," he said, exasperated, "now I'm doing *this.*"

"So they should be stopped before they wreak havoc?" she asked, sounding bored.

"They should be stopped because they tricked me. *Me!* I was top of my class at MIT!"

"I never would have guessed," she said, eyeing his tie, which was four inches wide at its broadest point. "So, you're tagging along—"

"Actually, I'm letting you tag along."

"Oh, please. And when you get this back, you'll give it to me?"

"Umm," he said, then darted out the garage door. "Come on, come on!"

She trudged after him. "I knew I should have gone back to bed when my semiauto jammed before breakfast."

"Can I drive?" He was circling her banana yellow convertible and caressing the leather seats.

"Forget it, Dr. Dork."

"It's Ben."

"Tara. Tara Marx."

"Of course it is," he said, and grinned at her. "Did anyone ever tell you, you're sort of like a Bond villain, except with great legs?"

"Christ," she muttered.

"Come to think of it, we should definitely take my car."

"Christ."

Three

Tara Marx tried to sneak looks at Dr. Dyson without being obvious. She couldn't believe it, but she'd let him talk her into taking his car. His dark green Dodge Neon. The geek-mobile. There was barely enough room for Katya, who was currently grooming herself in the backseat, never mind the two of them.

"I still don't understand why we couldn't take my Alfa Romeo."

"And I don't understand why the rat had to come with us."

"Don't talk about Katya like that. She's not 'the rat.' "

"Jeez, sorry, what is she, 'the duck'? Anyway, this baby is loaded with extras." Dyson actually patted the steering wheel, just in case she hadn't tumbled to what a gigantic geek he was. "You won't be sorry."

"I'm already sorry." She snuck another peek. It was the eyes; it wasn't her fault. Well, the eyes and the hair. The mussed dark red hair, which stood straight up as if he spent the day running his fingers through it. He needed a haircut; that's why he was so distracting and shaggy. She'd never seen hair that color before . . . so dark a red it was like mahogany.

No, the eye. The vivid, whiskey-colored eye (the other one

was blue). No, the stubble, blooming along his chin, that whole too-busy-to-shave thing was really sexy. No, the height, all rangy power—who would have thought a redheaded lab geek would have a swimmer's shoulders and a weight-lifter's legs?

She'd heard tales of *the* Dr. Dyson for years, and he certainly wasn't anything like she'd pictured him. Of course, you shouldn't put stock in stereotypes, but he was so far the opposite of one it was a joke, or a crime. He looked like an escapee from a *Hunky Men of Love* calendar, not a lab drone. And he'd been so outraged when she told him about Krueger & Co., he'd demanded he *come with her*. Most people would have called the cops. Or shrugged and gone back to work. Now she had a partner.

She did not play well with others.

"It's just," she tried again, "my car gets better gas mileage, among other things."

"Um," he said, or something like it. He was stabbing buttons on the dashboard—turning on the air conditioner?—and then the entire right-hand side of the windshield went opaque. Fortunately, his side stayed clear, or she would have been deeply, deeply concerned. Then the shield divided into grids and then resolved itself into a map. She could see two dots steadily moving and heard the light "ping-ping" of a radar system.

"Excellent," she managed. Dr. Dyson was years ahead of American technology, which wasn't so impressive, but he was also years ahead of the Germans, which was. "That'll work."

"Gotcha," he muttered, and stomped on the accelerator.

"Easy, big guy," she said, which was nothing but the truth—she was big, and almost never ran into taller men, but he had three inches on her, easily. Maybe that was it. It was so weird—and nice—to be with a guy who had some height on her. "I want to get them, too, but getting a ticket will slow you down. And be a major inconvenience to me, not that you care."

"Um," he said. Then he elaborated. "This car can see every radar gun in a five-mile radius." He pressed a button, and two orange blips appeared on the screen, far below their marked position. "We'll never get caught in a speed trap, if that's what you're worried about."

"That's not the only thing I'm worried about," she said under her breath, sneaking another peek. God, she had to get laid. It was the only explanation for why she was sitting in the passenger's side—the *passenger's* side!—of a Dodge Neon, lusting after a lab puke. A tall, handsome, stubbly, stubborn, antirat lab puke. "Where are we going?"

"After the bad guys," he responded, as if she was mildly retarded.

"I know *that*, Dyson. And then what?"

"Then, I take back what they tricked me out of."

"With what, the yogurt?" Maybe he'd run over them with his car. Dyson was built, sure, but those weren't field abs; that was a Bally's Swim and Fitness rack. Did he think March and Webber and Johanssen were going to hand it over if he asked nicely?

Well, fine. If rough stuff was coming up, she could handle it. Dyson was the brains; she'd be the muscle. Being able to quit The Biz would be infinitely easier if she got her hands on that card.

"They'll be sorry they *ever* showed me a fake Purchase Order," Dyson was yakking.

"You're acting like you didn't get paid."

"I did so get paid, and that's not the point. They lied. Like you said, everybody knows I don't make anything for the bad guys. They'll be sorry," he vowed again.

"Sure they will. How are we going to find them? Are you tracking them right now?"

"Uh-huh. I build STDs into all my gadgets."

"You infected all your gadgets with sexually transmitted diseases?"

"Grow up. Satellite Tracking Devices."

"Oh, *really*?"

"Well, sure."

"All of them."

"Umm."

"What an excellent way," she commented, "to get your head blown off. The first time anyone realizes you're tracking—"

"I've been doing this since high school—"

"Surprise, surprise."

"—and nobody's found one yet."

She smiled to herself.

"And now that I've told you," he joked, cutting the wheel to the right, "I'll have to kill you."

"That's probably best," she replied.

"Uh. I was only kidding."

"Then you're as dumb as you look." A rather large lie, but who cared? Lying was her best thing.

Well, second-best.

Four

"We've got them now," Ben chortled, turning into the parking lot. All right! The lair of the bad guys! Excellent, just excellent. They'd crash the den of evil and get his card back, and maybe bust a few bad guy skulls along the way. Yeah!

"Jenny's Flowers," Tara observed, reading the sign.

"The lair is a flower shop?"

"Maybe one of them has a girlfriend and wants to pick up a little something on the way home from thieving."

He snorted, which made Tara laugh again. "Cut that out, Dr. Dyson. It makes my stomach hurt."

"It's Ben. And it's not my fault you're an easy mark."

"Actually, I'm not. But speaking of easy marks, what's the plan?"

"What, you're asking me? You're the one with experience in this . . . stuff." He was dying to ask the statuesque beauty just how much of a villain she was. Robbing banks via the Internet villain, or pistol whipping while relieving the elderly of their social security check villain? Because he could live with one, but not the other. "You know, this sort of thing."

"Before you ask—and what a clumsily phrased question it would be, I'm sure—I'm Switzerland."

Yeah, probably. She certainly looked like she could come

from Switzerland. She looked like a badass milkmaid. "Okay."

"So, sometimes I work for the good guys and sometimes I work for the bad guys, but mostly I work for myself—and try to keep my head down."

Oh, she was *neutral* like Switzerland. Right. Hmm, he was definitely a little off today. Usually . . .

"I'm usually much quicker," he told her, which was stupid, because it was way too late to try to make a favorable first impression. "Honest."

"You could hardly be slower," was her heartless comment.

He was momentarily crushed, but quickly rallied. "You'll just have to take my word for it. So, do we just charge in there and start knocking skulls?"

"Dr. Dyson. Have you ever been in a fist fight?"

"Well, there was this one time in graduate school . . . My lab partner was late for the wet lab and the prof said it would affect both our grades . . . I got a little hot under the collar . . ."

"So, no."

"I fell down the stairs once and got a black eye," he confessed. "Does that count?"

She was rubbing her forehead as though she'd gotten a sudden migraine. "Should've stayed in bed . . . should've just stayed in bed . . ."

"Let's not talk about you being in bed; it's distracting."

"Pig," she commented, rolling her eyes.

"All that's changed now," he declared. He opened his car door and jumped out. "I'm not Q anymore, I'm James!"

"What?"

"For example, in my old life, I'd never have dared make that bed comment. But no longer!"

"What?"

"Never mind. Let's go kick some ass. They'll be sorry they messed with Benjamin Everett Dyson!"

"I'm sure they're shaking in their Dock Martens." Then, "Everett?"

He ignored the slur on his mother's maiden name and stomped up to the door of the flower shop, paused, then kicked it. It wheezed open a foot, then slowly shut.

"It's business hours," Tara pointed out. "They're open. See?" She eased the door open.

He darted inside, looking around wildly for a bad guy, any bad guy. "Everybody freeze!"

"For God's sake," Tara muttered, pushing past him.

"You," he said to the startled teenaged girl behind the counter. "Where is it?"

"Well, we have a special on roses. A baker's dozen for twenty-five ninety-nine."

"Don't play dumb," he sneered. "We know what you've been up to."

"For God's sake," Tara said again. "She's the front. She doesn't know anything."

"I am not," the girl said automatically. Then, "What's a front?" This was really good, because it saved Ben from having to ask the question and looking, well, stupid.

"This shop is a front. You're a front," Tara told her. "The guys you work for have to have some legitimate businesses to hide their money in."

"But I work for a woman. Katie Webber."

"Yeah, Webber bought this place as a present for his wife, but he didn't tell her he was gonna use it to launder money."

"How do you know all this?" Ben asked.

"There's a bad guy newsletter," she replied straight-faced.

"You guys are crazy," the girl declared.

Ben asked, "Why not a strip club or something a little more . . . I dunno . . . villainous?"

"Too much heat in the boob trade," Tara replied.

It was just fascinating how she knew all this cool stuff. Maybe there really *was* a newsletter. He had a million questions for her. Later. "Okay," he said to the kid behind the counter, who was looking increasingly freaked out, "did some guys come through here a while ago?"

"There's a back entrance," Tara said—okay, now it was getting downright spooky how she knew all this stuff. "This kid wouldn't have any idea if they were here or not, unless she went in the back and saw them."

"I'm not a kid," the girl corrected her. "I'm nineteen."

"How do you know all this?" Ben couldn't resist asking again.

"Every business establishment has a back door. Hello? Fire code?" She shook her head and looked at him as if his nose had dropped off.

"Why didn't you say anything *then?*" he said, exasperated.

"You didn't give me a chance, Dr. Charge In Without Looking."

"Look, we're just gonna go in the back and look around," he told the kid.

"Maybe I should call the police," she said doubtfully.

Ben looked at Tara, who shrugged. "What? I don't know from the police. That's not really my area."

"Maybe you should call them," he said.

"Sure, go ahead and call. But if they get the card before we do, it'll sit in the evidence room for a year and be called Exhibit A."

"Don't call the police," he told the girl.

"Look, are you guys going to buy roses or what?"

"That's a pretty good price," he said. "Sure, I'll take a bunch."

"Do you have Attention Deficit Disorder by any chance?" Tara asked. "You can tell me. I won't get mad or anything. I just want to know."

"Only since you showed up," he muttered, handing the kid two twenties.

Amazingly, Tara blushed . . . her pale cheeks bloomed

with color, and her eyes seemed to get darker. "That's not true. Is it? Of course not. Is it?"

"Who do you think I'm buying the stupid flowers for?"

"So we're going to run after the bad guys while I lug around a dozen flowers?"

"A baker's dozen," the girl said brightly, wrapping them up.

"For God's sake." Tara tried to scowl, but couldn't help a small smile when the girl handed her the dark red flowers. "Can we get back on track now, do you think?"

"I'm just gonna go over here and clean up the cooler," the girl said, pointing to the large glass case in the front of the store. "So I wouldn't know if you guys went into the back or anything. I mean, I still think you're nuts, but you can't do much damage in the back, unless you're arsonists."

"Well, we're not. Thanks," Ben told her. "Maybe you should get another job."

"Are you kidding? This is part-time, but I get full-time bennies. Plus dental. My mom's plan doesn't even do that."

"How nice for you," Tara commented.

"Tell me! Good luck with . . . you know, whatever it is you're doing."

"Thanks," Ben said. "Good luck with your flowers. And your dental."

Five

Dr. Dyson was creeping ahead of her, which was silly because he was making as much noise as an elephant in the brush. Tara walked behind him, lugging the gorgeous, stupid roses.

"Okay," he whispered, "here's what we're going to—"

"Anybody home?" Tara asked loudly.

"Ack! Don't *do* that. Stay behind me," he ordered, clutching his cell phone. "I'll take out anybody who tries something."

"Sure you will." Tara could see the body, which looked exactly like a huddled bunch of bloody rags, beneath one of the tables on the west side of the room. "Thataway, Dr. Dyson."

"Ben, Ben, do I have to write it on my chin?"

"That could be fun," she commented.

"Hey," he said, spotting the body, "somebody's in trouble."

"Okay, you can go with that theory." *Me, I'm thinking along the lines of good riddance.*

Before she could stop him (sigh), he raced over to the body and flipped it on its back. An excellent way to get shot in the face if the body wasn't really a body.

But this time, it was. Or damn near.

"It's Webber," she commented, surprised. The worst of them all, shot and left for dead. Wonders never ceased.

"Webber?" Ben whispered.

She decided to make a long story short. "Bad bad bad bad bad *bad* man."

The body opened its eyes, which were so bloodshot the whites weren't visible at all. Kaarl Webber tried to grin up at her, and failed.

"Marx," he wheezed.

"Kaarl," she said politely. Then, casting about for a way to continue the conversation (she sucked at small talk), she added, "Head shot, huh?"

"Stupid."

"Bound to happen," she commented.

"Lie still," Dyson said, flipping his cell open and tapping buttons. "I'm calling for help."

Tara promptly kicked the phone out of his hand, and he watched in amazement as it skidded across the cement floor.

"Thanks," Webber wheezed.

"No problem," she replied.

"What the *hell?*" Dyson snapped.

They ignored him. In truth, she didn't feel terribly sorry for Webber, who liked to trade heroin for the nightly use of little boys, but it was pathetic to watch him cling so desperately to life. A head shot, a chest shot, and it looked as if he'd been kneecapped, too. Not a nice way to die, and she wished he'd get on with it.

"Stupid," he was gasping. "Never thought they'd have the nerve. Double-cross *me.*"

"Try not to talk," Dyson begged.

"Where are they going?" she asked.

"Tara, what did I just *say?*"

"The Mayo," Webber whispered.

"Why?"

Ben said, "I think he wants us to take him to the Mayo

Clinic, which frankly is an excellent idea given the circumstances."

Webber ignored him. "Cure . . . for some kind of . . . cancer . . . steal . . . charge billions . . . to give back . . ."

"Sneaky," Tara said approvingly.

Webber didn't reply; he had died.

"He'll be avenged," Dyson vowed.

"For God's sake," Tara said. "This guy totally got what was coming to him." *Hell, I was thinking of doing him in myself.*

"Nobody has this coming," Dyson said, examining the head wound. "Christ. How he hung on long enough to have a conversation is a complete mystery."

Not really. Villains are really good at the whole cling-to-life-to-burn-ex-partners thing. "Yes, it's a total mystery. Well, at least now we know what the bad guys are up to." She paused, then asked hopefully, "I suppose this is too much blood and gore for a fellow like you, so how about you take the car and head back home and I'll—"

"Fuck that," Dyson said, which was startling, if kind of sexy. "We're going to the Mayo. Right now. I mean, as soon as I get my cell—there it is!"

"Of course we are," she said, watching him scoop up his phone from the far corner, then followed him out.

Six

"You realize it's about a two-hour drive to the Mayo. And it's kind of a big place. Like, university-campus big."

"I know," Ben replied, watching the tracking screen on the right side of the windshield. Yes, indeed, there they were, right where that poor shot fellow said they'd be. "We'll find them. Once we're on the highway, I can . . . there!" He popped the clutch, set the speedometer at just under ninety, and hit the cruise. Tara was momentarily pressed back into her seat, then recovered.

"And, naturally, crashing and dying isn't exactly a big worry."

"This car can see a collision coming a mile away—literally—and adjust accordingly."

"Of course it can. Soon everyone will have one. So, what's the plan when we get there? You can't exactly march into the Mayo. Well, you can, but eventually someone will ask you what you want."

"Hit the glove compartment button."

She obliged, and he noticed for the first time how long and pretty her fingers were, tipped, oddly, with Martian Green glitter nail polish. An odd choice for a thief, someone who wanted to blend in. Of course, she couldn't exactly blend, not with her height and hair and outfit. What was really weird was, he liked her for it.

He heard a faint nibbling coming from the backseat and deduced the rat was chewing on the roses. Dammit.

The glove box opened, and he said, "Lift the lid of the larger box."

She did, extracting two ID cards, freshly laminated. "Whoa," she said, examining them.

"You'll have to stick the what-do-you-call-'ems on . . . the clips. There's a box of them under your seat."

"Dr. Benjamin Dyson, Oncology. Dr. Jane Carlson, Oncology." Tara raised her eyebrows at him. "Dr. Jane Carlson?"

"Well, I didn't want to use your real name."

She laughed, and stuck the clips on, then put her fake Mayo employee badge on. "What makes you think Tara Marx is my real name?"

"Oh." Duh. "Right."

"How are we going to find the oncology department without asking a bunch of stupid questions?"

"I interned at the Mayo. Unless they've rearranged the entire building—always a possibility—I can find it. Besides, there's always the directories."

"You mean you're a *doctor* doctor?"

"Sure." She looked so surprised, it surprised *him*. "What?"

"A medical doctor?"

"Yeah. I got my MD a few years ago when I got bored. It didn't take very long."

"So you're an MD, and I heard you've got at least two PhDs . . ."

He coughed modestly. It was refreshing to share this with a beautiful woman; usually such glorious creatures weren't impressed by his credentials. And he couldn't tell them what he *really* did for a living. All the drawbacks of being a field agent, none of the perks. "Three, actually. Physics, organic chemistry, and explosives technology."

"I am sooooo turned on right now."

"Really?" he asked eagerly.

"No. Not really."

His shoulders slumped. "Yeah, I figured. Well, listen, Tara—if that is your *real* name—"

"I just told you it wasn't."

"—we've got a long drive, and we'd better pass the time. So, what brings you to law breaking?"

"A broken home."

"Really?"

"No. Not really."

"Gonna be a long ride," he muttered.

"Not really," she said, yawning. She snuggled back into the car seat and closed her eyes. In another minute her head was leaning against the passenger side window, and she was breathing evenly.

"Tara?"

No reply.

"Come on, nobody falls asleep that fast. Tara?"

Nothing. She was out. Zonked.

"Well, shoot," he muttered, and inched the car up to ninety-five.

Seven

"Have a nice nap?"

"Lovely." She didn't expect someone like Ben Dyson to understand, when you were in the field you slept whenever and wherever you could. Over the years she'd been able to train herself to fall asleep at the snap of a pair of fingers . . . sometimes quicker. Now she felt alert, refreshed, and horny. No, just alert and refreshed.

"Will it be all right in the car?" he whispered as they walked up the sidewalk. His breath tickled her ear, which should have been annoying, but was really quite pleasant.

" 'It' has a name. Katya. And she'll be fine. She can take care of herself, believe me. Also, she's not in the car; she's in the pocket of my lab coat."

"What!" Dyson nearly tripped over a flower bed. He straightened and ran his fingers through his vibrant hair, making it stand up more crazily in all directions. She almost snickered. "Tara! We're supposed to be inconspicuous. And even under the best of circumstances, you don't exactly blend in."

"What's that supposed to mean?" she cried, stung.

"Tara, you have a skull and crossbones piercing your left nostril."

"So? *You're* wearing a brown tie. And at least I remembered to put both my contacts in, blue eye."

"Leave the tie out of this. And the contacts." He paused outside the door to the clinic, took a deep breath, and said, "Okay, let's get it together."

"Yes, let's."

"Here we go."

"Thanks for stating the obvious again."

He glared at her, which almost made her laugh again, and held the door open. She swept past him, the hem of her lab coat flapping. It was actually a spare of his, and she'd had to roll the sleeves up. It smelled like him, too, a combination of Drakkar Noir cologne and clean cotton. She fought the urge to cuddle into it.

Memo to me: long past time to get laid. Once this is taken care of, take care of that.

She followed him to a set of elevators, and neither of them said a word as the car ascended several floors. At the appropriate floor, he grabbed her hand and walked out.

"How could they steal a cure for cancer?" Tara wondered aloud. "Like there aren't a ton of lab notes and computer files and stuff? They can't recreate it?"

"Maybe they're stupid bad guys," Dyson suggested.

"Well, they've stayed a step ahead of you pretty handily."

"Us," he said, glaring.

"Oh, sure."

"This way," he said, turning left down a corridor.

"How the hell are they even still in the hospital?" she asked. "They should have grabbed what they needed and gotten out."

"Do you know what the cure for cancer looks like? Could you pick it out of a laboratory filled with beakers and fridges and tables and drawers and notes?"

"No," she admitted, "but I had sex in high school. I've always got that to cling to."

"I hate you," he sighed.

"Probably shouldn't have tagged along, then," she said smugly.

They paused outside a closed door that was lettered ACUTE LYMPHOCYTIC LEUKEMIA (ALL). "What's that?" she asked.

"Cancer of white blood cells." He was squinting at the wooden door and fumbling in his back pocket. "There's three guys in there."

"How do you know *that?*"

"This contact," he said, tapping the eye socket beneath his blue eye, "sees in X-ray."

"Of course it does." Still, she was impressed in spite of herself. She'd never met a guy so smart and so dumb at the same time.

She put her hand in her own pocket, gave Katya a pat, then asked, "Do you want me to kick the door in?"

"God, no. I've got a spare key card."

"You've got *what?*" she asked, staring as he withdrew a silver card the size of her Visa. "All this time you've had a spare?" Her fingers itched to strangle him. To choke him and stroke him and pull his shirt off . . . *no,* to slap the shit out of him and throw him out the window. "What the hell am I doing here, then?"

"Well," he said reasonably, "if you knew there was a spare skeleton card, you wouldn't have helped me."

"Damned right I wouldn't have helped you!"

"Shhhhhhh!"

She seized him by the collar and began to shake him back and forth. Ohhhh, the things she would do. Tendons would rip; muscles would tear. She'd wrap that stupid brown tie around his throat and choke him until his multicolored eyes bulged out. She'd . . .

. . . kiss him back.

Somehow, during the attempted throttle, he'd gotten his arms around her and dodged her flying elbows and pulled her close. His mouth was moving over hers, and he smelled, oh, he smelled wonderful, and she was still clutching his collar, but now she was leaning into him, into his mouth, into the kiss, the amazing, unbelievable kiss. . . .

He pulled back. "Whoa. Sorry, Tara."

"Huh?" she huhed.

"I mean, there's a time and place. It's just . . . I've wanted to do that since you marched into my garage. I mean my lab. And are you a *bad* bad guy? I mean, you don't beat up old ladies, do you?"

She was having a little trouble following the conversation. "What? No. What?"

"Oh, good. Because we can work on the rest."

"What?"

"Well, let's get in there, then."

She grabbed his shoulder and spun him back, then planted one on his mouth for good measure. She'd call the shots around here, thank you very much! If there was kissing, *she'd* be the kisser, not the kissee. Ooh, yeah, and now his hands were sliding up, caressing her back, and . . .

"Holy shit, it's Tara Marx!"

. . . the bad guys had opened the door.

Eight

"I told you," Ben said, trying not to sound smug. Trying not to sound out of breath, too. "I told you: time and place."

"Hi, March," Tara said. "Webber sends his regards. Okay, not really."

The beefy black man who opened the door jerked his head at Ben. "Whatcha got L.F. here for?"

Ben blinked. "L.F.?"

"Er, Lovely Friend," Tara said.

"Oh, no!" he said, horrified. "It's Lab Freak, isn't it? Isn't it!"

"Uh, yeah. But it's like a compliment."

"We paid you," the man named March said. Rumbled, actually. He was a full head taller than Ben, and about twice as wide. He'd be frightening enough without the shoulder-length dreads. "What's the problem?"

"Um, you lied and didn't mention you're going to use my invention to screw over my country?"

"Yeah," Tara added.

"Oh, like *you* give a shit," March snapped at her. He was dressed in splendid bad guys' fashion—black suit, black shoes, black shirt, black tie, black tie clip.

"I've got my reasons."

"Yeah, yeah, don't cry about it again. 'One more big job and I'm out; one more payoff and I'm going straight.' Puke."

Ben turned to her, surprised. She looked, weirdly, embarrassed. "Really, Tara? Good for you."

"Oh, shut up," she muttered. "You shut up, too, March. Are you gonna let us in, or do I have to kick your big butt up and down this corridor?"

"You're gonna have to kick my big butt up and down this corridor. And watch it with the weight comments," he added, wounded. "I've been working out."

"Fine," Tara said, and Ben almost gasped. Gorgeous, a great kisser, smelled like a meadow, and she was fearless, besides! What a woman! "It's on!"

"No, you don't," he said, grabbing her shoulder and thrusting her behind him. He whipped out his cell phone and pointed it at the enormous man in the doorway, a man so large he was actually turned sideways in order to fit. "Don't touch her or you'll be sorry."

March blinked. "What, you're gonna call your mama?" Then he said, "Eeaarrrgggghhhhh!" as an electric current shot from the phone into his chest. He twitched a few times like the world's largest bass, then collapsed in the doorway. They had to skip back to avoid being crushed.

"And I'll bet it works as a phone, too," Tara commented, watching March fall.

"Of course it does," he replied, offended.

"You are a weird weird man," she commented. "Well, that's two bad guys out of three. Got any other tricks up your sleeve?"

"You'll see," he said with bravado that was, amazingly, entirely unfaked. Being in the field was exactly as exciting and as much fun as he imagined! "Let's go."

"Okay," she said, and kicked his legs out from under him, then jumped on top of him. A bullet smacked into the wall where his chest had been a fraction of a second earlier.

"I didn't know you cared," he said, staring into her green-ish eyes.

"I'd just hate to see the hallway get all messed up," she said, flinching as a bullet whined overhead. "At least he's using a silencer. Otherwise we'd have tons of company up here."

"He's shooting at us?"

"Not everyone buys flowers." She snickered, then rolled over, pulling him into a sheltered corner of the hallway. "Don't worry, it won't take long. He doesn't like walking around with spare clips—says it wrecks the line of his suit."

"So he's just gonna shoot blindly until it's empty?"

"Sure. He has no idea who's after him, so it's a relatively sound plan. Wouldn't *you* run?"

"I would not!"

"Fine, fine. Just stay down."

"You know, bad guys trying to blow my head off isn't as much fun as I thought it would be," Benjamin commented. "It's more stressful than anything else."

"Typical," Tara said. "Felony assault—it's all hype."

"Any bright ideas on how to get out of this?"

"Ben, I am *so* not the brains of this team. Besides, it's your fault we're even here."

"The hell! You're the one who wanted to steal the world."

"I didn't want to steal the *world,* just a few key pieces of it, not that it's any of your business. *You're* the one who in-sisted we save humanity." Tara invested the phrase with heavy sarcasm. "Could there be a bigger waste of time? No? Ask the guys with the guns if you don't believe me."

"Fine. Anyway, we'd better get out of here before bullets start exploring our temporal lobes. This hallway isn't going to provide cover much longer."

"So? Think of something, gadget man." Tara stretched out her long, long legs and closed her eyes. "Let me know what you come up with."

He watched, dumbfounded, as she went to sleep. She could always do that. It was unbelievably aggravating.

He leaned over and shouted into her gorgeous, still face, "And I did *not* get us into this!" In the distance, the firing pop of the silencer accentuated his statement.

"Did, too," Tara said without opening her eyes.

"Did not!"

"Don't you remember?"

As a matter of fact, he did. "Never mind that," he snapped. He counted another three shots, which added up to nine. "Hey, he's all done. We can storm the bridge, so to speak."

He started to get up, only to feel Tara grab his ankle—in her sleep, apparently—and pull him back down, just in time for another bullet to whine overhead. "Nine in the clip, one in the pipe," she said without opening her eyes.

"I knew that," he lied. Actually, he hardly ever messed around with guns. Dull, dull, dull. It was more fun to mess around with cell phones and car engines.

"Of course you did." She yawned and sat up. "Ready?"

"If you're all done catnapping."

"Don't knock it. I'm fresh as a daisy while you're just . . . well, never mind."

"Stay behind me," he ordered her. "I'll look out for you."

"Great. I'm sure I'll enjoy my early grave." But she waited for him to jump through the doorway over March's still unconscious frame, then followed.

Nine

The final confrontation was anticlimactic, to say the least.

Johanssen blinked at both of them and, as a terrified-looking physician cowered behind a counter, said, "What are you two doing here? And what in the world did you do to March?"

"We're here to *stop* you!" Dyson declared, and Tara rolled her eyes. Since she'd hooked up with Ben Dyson, it seemed that's what she did most of the time. "Just like we put a stop to March and his nefariousness!"

"I'm not really with him, Jo," she explained. "Well. I'm *with* him, but not *with* him with him."

"What, you've got a problem all of a sudden?" Johanssen was looking puzzled, thank goodness, as opposed to homicidal, which would have been very bad. She couldn't really blame him. They'd never had to cross paths before. In a weird sort of way, she respected him. Well. She had until she found the body at the florist's. "Why? Why now?"

"Because you're a deceiver and you're going to hurt thousands of Americans!"

"Ben. Let. Me. Handle. This."

"Dr. Dyson, what do you think you're doing?" Johanssen was a deceptively mild looking man in his fifties, with dark eyes netted with wrinkles ("laugh lines," for someone who laughed), a medium build, and tough, blocklike hands. His suit proclaimed "businessman." His hands said something else.

Ben shook his cell phone, which she suspected was currently lacking a charge, at Jo. "Stopping you, you foul fiend of—of—evil!"

"Foul fiend of evil?" Tara repeated.

"You got paid, right?" he asked, still sounding puzzled.

"Irrelevant!"

"Wh-what's going on?" the doc shivering behind Johanssen squeaked. He was a smallish man with watery blue eyes, a pale blond combover, and a neck so weirdly long he reminded her of a chicken. "Who are you people?"

"Never mind," Johanssen said absently. "I'll take care of it."

"I didn't sign on for any of this when I hired you," squeaky doc continued.

Tara rolled her eyes again. Civilians, swear to God. Sweat them a little, ramp up the pressure, and they spilled their guts.

"You hired him to steal my key card?"

"We didn't steal anything," Jo explained patiently. "We paid you."

"You paid me . . . in subterfuge!"

Tara started to massage her temples. "God . . . God . . . God . . ."

"Well, you don't work for criminals," Jo said. "You're famous for your naïve patriotism. So we had to pay you in, er, subterfuge."

"I'm dying to know," Tara confessed. "How'd you make the paperwork look right?"

"My brother-in-law is a clerk for the CIA," Combover volunteered. Jo's mouth thinned, but he let the doc babble on. "He showed me samples of POs and stuff."

"Did he know what you were going to do?" Dyson asked, appalled.

"Well . . . he wants to borrow the card for a weekend at work . . ."

Note to self: find brother-in-law and clean his clock. "Look, Jo," Tara said, "I'm really sorry, but we're gonna have to get that card back. We just, um, can't let you or this guy run around with it. So, uh, let's not have a problem, okay?"

"Sorry, Tara."

"*You're* the one who's going to be sorry," Dyson declared.

"I just *said* I was sorry," Jo snapped back.

"You don't know how sorry," Dyson sneered. "This gorgeous blonde to my left is deadly in the field."

"Awww," Tara said. *Gorgeous? That's so sweet.*

"Oh, I know," Jo said.

Dyson nodded, looking triumphant. "Her fiendish reputation precedes her, eh?"

"Actually," Tara confessed, "he's sort of my mentor."

"Your *what?*"

"Taught her everything she knows," Jo boasted. "Practically raised her."

"Not everything," she said coolly. "For example, you didn't teach me to shoot my partner and leave him for dead while you ran off with the goods."

"Why would I teach you *that?* Do I look like I want a head wound anytime in my future?"

"I have to say, I'm disappointed, Jo." And she was. In the old days, he'd never have left a body. If for no other reason than it was messy. "Seriously."

"You're a child, Tara," he said, kindly enough. "You always were. You think you're bad, but at the center you're softer than a marshmallow egg. It's why you'll never be great."

"Great like you?" she sneered.

"Good parting line," Dyson said. "Get him!"

"Well, just a minute."

"Why?" Ben asked. "What are you waiting for?"

"Look, the guy's got about a million black belts, okay? And who do you think taught *me* how to fight?"

"Actually, I've never seen you fight," he pointed out, "but I'm assuming you know what you're doing."

"Did she say you killed someone?" Dr. Combover asked, finally catching up. "I didn't sign on for that! You were supposed to get the card, that's all, just get the card!"

"Collateral damage," Jo sniffed.

"We'll show *you* collateral damage," Ben said. He stuck his hand in his pocket, withdrew the blackberry yogurt he'd grabbed earlier, and lobbed it, grenade-style, at Jo.

It splattered all over the floor, Jo's shoes, and his trouser legs. Tara waited expectantly for Jo to melt or blow up or fall down unconscious, but nothing happened.

"You've ruined my suit," Jo commented, leaning down to brush purple puree off his pants.

"What's in it?" Tara breathed. "What's going to happen?"

"Nothing. It's just yogurt," Ben muttered to her.

"*Now* you tell me." She sighed, then waded in. Getting her ass kicked sideways by her mentor wasn't on her list for the day, but what the hell. She certainly couldn't let Ben take him on. Jo would eat him for lunch, spit out the bones, and bury them in some far-off field.

"Left leg!" Ben ordered, squinting.

Tara obligingly kicked out at Jo's left leg, and Jo obligingly moved, sweeping her blow aside. "Easier said than done," she said over her shoulder, and then her ears rang as Jo punched her head. Which she totally deserved; what had she been thinking, taking her eyes off the ball?

Everything went sort of blurry for a second, and there was a high-pitched whining sound, followed by the more recognizable sound of Ben yelling, "You son of a bitch!"

"Don't," she managed, only to be knocked sprawling as he surged past her and jumped on Jo.

Jo went down—he was well trained, but Ben was a big

guy—but rallied quickly by grabbing Ben's tie, doubtless meaning to strangle Ben to death (a compulsion she well understood). Instead he shrieked and let go of the tie and stared at the blood pouring down his hand.

"Ha!" Ben crowed. "Never touch the tie!" He punched Jo square in the face—Tara could hear the flat smacking sound of flesh hitting flesh—and let out a howl. "Aiiggh! That hurts!"

Jo turned his head to the side, spat out a tooth, then sneered, "You watch too many movies, Dr. Dyson." Then he didn't say anything, because there was a "bronnnnnnggggg!" as he was knocked unconscious with a microscope.

By Dr. Combover.

"He wasn't supposed to kill anybody," the doctor said dully, dropping the microscope on the counter. "I didn't—he wasn't supposed to do that."

Ben leaped to his feet. "Good work. We'll be sure to tell the police about your last-second change of heart."

"Yeah, we'll mention that right away," Tara said. "And what's with your tie? Your stupid, too-wide, brown tie?"

"It's lined with throwing stars," he explained. "I forged them out of titanium so they'll never—"

"Forget I asked. Why'd you do it?" she said to Combover, who, according to his ID, was Dr. Krendall. "You work here, right? We were told Jo was stealing a cure. Did you hire Jo and his team to steal it for you?"

"A . . . cure? Stealing a cure? No . . . no. I'm close, but . . . no. He might have told his men that, I don't know. It's . . . I'm stalled on my research," he said, staring at the floor. "Between my boss and the FDA and . . . I just know I could make some real progress if I could get into the other labs . . . and Mr. Jones told me with this new card the computer wouldn't track me, nobody would know I was here or what I was doing . . . You have no idea how the FDA can slow you down . . ."

"Yeah, they're so pesky with their rules to guarantee

safety," Dyson said, glaring. "There's a dead guy, and you're going to jail so your rep is in shreds, and any chance for a cure is stalled indefinitely, and for what?"

"For a cure," Combover said simply. "A cure is worth anything. Everything."

Tara didn't know about that; she wasn't the brains of this operation, for sure. But it sure seemed like an awful lot of waste. Ben was right . . . for what?

Ten

"That's it?" Ben was asking. "That's all? It's so . . . so . . ."

"Over?" Tara suggested.

"Shouldn't we at least wait until the police—"

"Pass."

"Oh. Well, all right. I guess they aren't going anywhere. How many handcuffs do you normally carry on your person, anyway?"

"That's for me to know," she said smugly, "and you to find out."

"You know, when you tried to take out Johanssen . . . your mentor . . . to help me . . . that was really great."

"Why'd you yell about his left leg?"

"I could see it was a badly mended break," he said, pointing to his blue eye.

"Oh. Creepy."

"Sort of the way I can see you're wearing a demi-cup bra," he said, grinning.

"I don't know what's worse, that you're ogling me with your fake contact lens or that you know the word 'demi-cup'." They were striding—not running, but not lingering, either—toward the west exit, when she suddenly grabbed his arm and hustled him into an empty hospital room. "Want to know what color it is?"

"Cherry red," he said without hesitation.

She gasped. "How'd you know that?"

"Trade secret."

She snapped the lock closed on the door, shrugged out of her lab coat, and pulled her shirt over her head. "Well, ding ding ding," she said. "You get the prize."

"What a day," he said dreamily, then grabbed her around the waist and kissed her until she was out of breath.

They found themselves on the (fortunately empty) bed, and for the first time all day Tara felt as if time wasn't her enemy, as though she could do as she pleased for as long as she liked. She got him out of his coat, got the tie off (very carefully; it was so sharp there was no visible blood on it), got the shirt off, and was fumbling for his belt buckle when he pushed the cups of her bra down and kissed her breasts. She forgot about his belt—and everything else—as he licked and sucked her nipples, as he ran his knuckles across the full undersides of her breasts, as he kissed her cleavage.

"You're so gorgeous," he said, raising his head to look her in the eye.

"Inside and out?" she teased.

He laughed and bent back to her cleavage, and she ran her fingers through his wild red hair. "This is nuts," she sighed. "The police are on the way, if they aren't already here."

"This hospital is huge," he said, his voice muffled. "It'll take them a while to get to us, if they even make it to this wing."

"And what about Katya?"

"She's having Cheez Nips in the bathroom; she's in heaven. I knew stopping by the snack machine on the way out was going to pay off . . ."

She whipped his belt out of the loops and sent it sailing across the room, then wriggled out of her pants and helped him out of his—

"These hospital blankets are scratchy," he complained.

—and rolled over until she was on top of him. He reached up and unlatched her bra, then sighed happily when her breasts bounced free. "What a day," he sighed again.

She trailed kisses down his neck, his chest—broad and furred with reddish brown hair—then inhaled his male musk and ran her tongue along the length of his throbbing penis. He groaned and tried to bury his hands in her hair—it was too short—and settled for fondling her earlobes instead.

She sucked his tip into her mouth and let her tongue play across its velvety head, marveling at the size of him, the warmth, his good clean smell.

"Oh, God," he gasped. "Please don't stop. Ever."

"For anything?" she teased, stripping off her panties and straddling him. He reached between her thighs and found her slippery, and she squirmed against his fingers as he stroked and teased.

"By the way," he sighed as she lowered herself on top of him, "it really turned me on when you punched Dr. Krendall in the kidneys to get him to give us his brother-in-law's name."

"Thanks," she said, almost moaned, as she settled herself over him. Oh, Christ, that's what she needed, that's what was missing. She began to rock against him as he gripped her hips and thrust against her.

"Tara . . . oh, God . . . Tara . . ."

She leaned down and nipped the side of his neck as he thrust faster; he reached between her legs and found her clit again and stroked it with the barest of butterfly strokes, and that delicate touch, coupled with the sweet size of him thrusting inside her, brought her to orgasm, made her close her eyes and shiver with the glory of it.

"Come now," she said, almost pleaded, and he wrapped his strong arms around her and pumped against her, and obliged.

* * *

Later, in the gloom of the room, they reassembled their clothes and tried to get their breath back. Tara was having a hard time looking at Ben; she felt curiously shy. It wasn't like her at all to just jump some stranger's bones. Except Ben didn't feel like a stranger. And wasn't that odd? They'd known each other . . . what? Five hours?

Trying to get her mind back on business, she peeked out the window but only had a view of the next building; she couldn't see any cop cars.

He came up behind her and dropped a kiss to her neck. She shivered and leaned back against him. It was odd. Very very odd. She should be anxious to be gone. But all she wanted was to go home with him and rent movies and make out on the couch and sleep late the next morning.

"Ready to sneak out of Dodge?" he teased. "The Damon parking ramp is a couple of buildings away."

"Sure."

"I'll get the rat."

She paused, then said, "Janet. My real name is Janet."

Now it was his turn to pause. He turned her around, kissed her softly, then said, "Thank you."

She had no reply; what else was there to say?

Eleven

Ben sighed, stretched, and rolled over to grope for her. What a day! What a night! After she'd insisted on renting movies, she'd been unstoppable in the sack. Not that he had tons of sack experience. But still. She'd been something else. Now he'd make her breakfast—well, take her out for breakfast—and they could spend the day together, like two ordinary people in—

She was gone.

He sat bolt upright. "T—Janet?" he called, knowing it was useless; his house had the familiar feel of emptiness to it. "Janet?"

He rolled out of bed, jumped into a pair of cutoffs, and quickly searched the house. Nobody home but him. Even the rat was gone.

He couldn't believe it. The day they'd spent together had been amazing enough, but the night had been . . . well . . . magical. She'd been alternately urgent and tender, and he'd been more than happy to meet her needs. Afterward, drifting off with her head on his shoulder, he'd felt like the happiest man who'd ever escaped from a lab.

Well, she was . . . she was an independent woman. A free spirit. And they'd just met, after all. Maybe she needed to, um, water her plants or whatever. It's not like they promised each other anything. It's not like he had something . . .

. . . something she wanted.

Oh, shit.

It took him forty seconds to ascertain that she had taken both key cards. He stormed up and down his lab, running his fingers through his hair, cursing himself for being ten kinds of a fool. He was an idiot! Of course she didn't like *him;* of course she wasn't going to stay with someone like *him.* She wanted the key card, and she got exactly what she came for.

God, the things he'd said to her! "You're so beautiful; you're so wonderful." His face burned with anger and embarrassment. She'd played him like a real chump. And she'd been right to do it . . . He *was* a chump.

Dr. Ben Dyson, Chump.

Fuck.

Twelve

"Dr. Dyson, we're getting to be sort of friends, don'tcha think?"

Ben, who had just returned from the grocery store, put the nachos and Coke away. Bemused, he watched Agent Tom Carradine shift his weight from one foot to another and case the place with his peripheral vision. "Friends? Well, uh . . ." *You come over. You drop off a check. You take what I made. You leave. A few months later, you come over again. Rinse. Repeat.* "Sure. Okay."

"Well, we're just—I mean, my supervisor and I—we were talking and—is everything all right?"

"No."

"Oh." Tom blinked, then tried again. "I could maybe arrange for you to talk to someone if there's, you know, a problem."

"No."

"Okay." Tom switched tactics. Ben would have been amused if he wasn't so fucking depressed. "Listen, word's out, you know, small world and all, and we heard you did some great work a few weeks back. And my supervisor could talk to the DCI and maybe get you into the next class at Langley."

How nice. Everything he ever wanted. Before he had a clue what he wanted. "No." He added, because it seemed like the polite thing to do, "But thanks."

"Well, how about if we get you into DI? With your skills and background, no problem."

Directorate of Intelligence. Analyst. Solving puzzles all day. Yawn. "No thanks."

"Okay, well, you sure you don't want to talk about it?"

"What do you want, Tom?"

Agent Carradine shrugged. "Just to see how you're doing."

"Oh. You don't need anything?"

"Just for you to get back on track. Everybody's noticed. You've been . . . off . . . for almost a month."

"Yeah, well. Thanks for checking in." Ben was almost—but not quite—touched. He performed a necessary function, after all, and people were bound to notice when he didn't do it anymore. He didn't like to admit, not even to himself, but the heart had gone right out of him around the time Janet had gone out of his house, never to return. Janet probably wasn't her real name, either, he supposed. "I'll see you."

"Sure. You've got my card, right?"

"About a dozen of them."

"Well, give me a shout if you want to talk."

"Sure."

"Take 'er easy."

"Ummm."

Tom left. Ben stored the extra nachos on top of the fridge. He thought about having a Coke, then changed his mind. Instead, he wandered through his empty house. Something was a little off, but it was probably fallout from Tom's visit. It didn't mean—

He could see a light beneath his bathroom door.

Normally he would have dived into his lab and grabbed the gadget *du jour* and kicked the door open and had a helluva good time. Now he just pushed the door open with tented fingers.

Tara was sitting on the end of the tub, which was full, wearing his bathrobe. "Finally," she said by way of greeting. "I didn't think that spook would ever leave."

He gaped at her.

"Sorry I'm late," she added. "I got held up at work. Okay, not really."

"How did you get—never mind." She had his key cards, after all, but he'd find out later how she'd avoided tripping any of the perimeter alarms. "W-what are you doing here?"

She crossed her legs and swung her left foot while she watched him. "Isn't it obvious?"

"Uh—no."

"I thought you were some kind of genius," she teased.

"Uh . . ."

"I had some things to take care of. Some accounts to close, some money to move, and I had to make the Tara Marx ident disappear. And I had something of yours to give back."

It almost sounded like she . . . but that was ridiculous. "Did you forget something on your way out?" he asked politely.

She winced. "Okay, I totally had that coming. Look, I freaked out for a little bit, okay?"

"What'd you use my cards for?"

"Nothing."

"Liar."

"I never lie." She paused. "Okay, that was a lie. But I was all set to use them, to do one last job, and I just . . . I thought about your stupid fat tie and your dopey multicolored eyes and your messy hair, and I realized it was a bad thing, leaving, and I wanted to make it right."

He worked hard not to show anything on his face, and was pretty sure he succeeded. "Really. And it took you a month to 'make it right.' "

"Be fair. I woke up that morning perfectly content with my old life, and by the end of the day I wanted something totally different. Well, I couldn't just drop everything and go into it overnight. I had people to explain things to. I had some work to finish, and some things to—to give back. I didn't want you involved in any of that. And I knew if I told you—well, you know."

"Did you give back all your telephones?" he asked, still polite. "Is that why you didn't call even one time?"

"I'll go," she said stiffly, standing.

"Dressed like that?"

"I'm sorry. I'm not used to people caring either way when I leave. I should have—never mind. I guess it's too late. For what it's worth, I guess I went about this all wrong."

She tried to move past him, and he took her (carefully!) by the arms. "I'm just surprised, is all. I was sort of getting used to you being gone," he lied. "And frankly, not knowing where the rat is, is freaking me out."

She smiled a little. "Katya, for God's sake. And she's in your other bathroom, taking a nap in the tub."

"The empty tub, one hopes."

"Look, Ben, enough about the rat."

"Katya," he corrected her.

"Right, right. Can I stay, or what?"

"You want to stay?" he asked carefully.

"No, I ran out of rent money."

"Really?"

"No." She smiled. "Not really."

"If you stay, that means you're going to stay."

"Like, what, a golden retriever?"

"I mean it, Janet. If you stay, it means I don't wake up alone and you're here for good and we're Dr. and Mrs. Dyson."

"And I make banana bread while you design gadgets for the FBI?"

"If you've got a thing for banana bread, fine, go crazy." She had popped open the first button of his shirt and was nibbling on the hollow of his throat, which made it difficult to remember what he was trying to say. "I just thought . . . um . . . we could be . . . ah . . . a team. Because I, um, love you."

"Great minds think alike," she murmured, popping open more buttons. "I don't love you at all, but you've got a nice house and I'm tired of being a nomad. Okay, not really. Ahhhh, there are the shoulders I remember. Dr. Dyson, has anyone ever told you, you have a fabulous body?"

"Tom never mentioned it," he said. He untied the belt of her—his—robe and spread it open. "Umm. Speaking of fabulous . . ." He leaned forward and kissed her.

She wrapped her arms around his neck and clung to him for a minute, then whispered, "I'm sorry."

"It's all right."

"No, I was an asshole."

"Umm."

"I'll fix it," she vowed, "if it takes twenty years."

"That's a deal, Janet." He pushed the robe off her shoulders and stepped into her, forcing her to back up until she was sitting on the tub. He knelt, pushed her knees wider and kissed her inner thighs, then inhaled her sweet musk and spread her lower lips apart with his tongue. He licked and sucked and felt himself grow painfully hard as her moans did to him what her taste did, as she gripped the sides of the tub and thrust her hips against his face. He sucked her clit into his mouth and teased it with his tongue until she was almost sobbing his name.

"Get over here," she said when he backed off. "Right now."

He had suddenly grown an extra five fingers, because getting his belt loose and his pants down had become nearly impossible. He finally staggered toward her, kicking free of his pants and fumbling for his boxers when her hand darted inside the fly vent and she seized him.

"Watch this," she said, standing and sounding as if she'd just run a marathon. "This is where being tall really comes in handy." Then she went up on her toes, and he slid inside her as if they had been designed for each other. "Oh, God. That's so nice. Don't stop."

"Right," he panted. "Because I was planning to do just that."

"Shut up and fuck me, Dr. Dyson."

"Call me Ben."

"Shut up and—oh! Oh, God, I'm going to—to—" She writhed against him, and thank goodness, because that about did it for him, he came so hard he saw black dots in front of his eyes. His knees bucked and she let out a little shriek as they fell backward into the tub.

Wriggling and squirming, they both surfaced. "Thank God you've got one of those big ones," she gasped.

"Why, thank you."

"Don't be an ass," she said, but she laughed as she tried to struggle free of his embrace. "God, there's water everywhere. We're gonna need fifty mops."

"Later."

"Well . . . I *am* feeling a little dirty . . ."

"Me, too," he sighed, and kissed her again and groped for the bar of soap.

ANYTHING YOU CAN DO . . .

Karen Kelley

Five

Alex shifted the small package to his other hand and dug around in the pocket of his sweats until he came up with the key to the apartment. His arm cramped. He massaged it as he inserted his key. Why the hell had he bought the stupid weights in the first place? Kagen might have drooled for all of two seconds. He hadn't impressed her with his manly form.

He turned the key in the lock and pushed the door open.

Heat slapped him in the face like a furnace door left open. Had the AC gone out? He tossed his package and keys onto a small entry table and glanced around the room.

That's when he saw Kagen stretched out on the sofa. The red bikini left little to the imagination.

She ran an ice cube across her lips, where she stole a slow lick, then down her chest and over her flat abdomen.

"It's so hot in here," she stated in a husky voice as a drop from the melting ice ran down to her bikini bottoms to be absorbed into the silky material. "I opened the windows to air the apartment—paint fumes—and turned the AC off. I just didn't realize it would get so warm."

He kicked the door closed and strode to the thermostat. A knowing grin crossed his face.

"You turned the heater on," he said as he adjusted the controls to the way they were before she'd meddled with them.

"I did? Imagine that."

"Yes, imagine that." He pulled his shirt over his head and tossed it onto the chair as he sauntered toward her once again. When he reached her, she looked at him with the expression of a woman who'd just beat her adversary.

Too bad she hadn't.

He leaned down and took the ice from her fingers, running it across his chest. "You're right, this is better." The ice actually did feel good when he ran the dissolving cube over his sore muscles.

She stood. He caught the exotic fragrance she seemed to prefer wearing. He inhaled, letting the scent fill him.

"If you want, I can massage *all* your body with ice," she whispered.

"Fire and ice. A deadly combination. If I didn't know better, I'd think you were tempting me."

She shrugged, and the strap on her bathing suit fell off her shoulder. He reached to replace it but drew his hand back at the last minute.

"All's fair in love and war." She slipped the strap back in place. "You might as well give in. You will eventually. Why put yourself through this torture? We could be so good together."

His gaze roamed over her. Her nipples strained against the thin, red material. As if to make sure he wouldn't miss a thing, she ran her hands across her breasts, lightly trailed down her abdomen, and grasped her thighs, biting her bottom lip. Ever so slowly, she moved her hands back up, scraping her fingers through her blond hair.

Alex drew in a shaky breath. Why in the hell didn't he give in? There had to be a perfectly good reason not to . . . He just couldn't think what it was right now. The only thing on his mind was Kagen, standing before him like a wanton sex goddess waiting for him to make slow, sensuous love to her.

In a daze, he lowered his mouth toward her lips. Just before he closed his eyes and kissed her something sparkled on her little finger. He frowned. On her pinkie was a tiny diamond ring twinkling up at him. A vision of a ten-year-old Lisa came rumbling across his mind like a storm cloud.

"Swear, Alex." She held up her pinkie.

He followed suit and spit on his finger as she'd done and touched her pinkie.

She grinned. "We'll never, ever break a promise to each other. Not if we pinkie-swear."

Damn! Kagen almost had him.

"I'll fulfill all your fantasies," she whispered as she raised up on her toes to meet his lips the rest of the way.

He took a deep, cleansing breath and stepped back. She lost her balance and fell forward. He caught her. Kagen's supple body landed against him. It wasn't her slight weight that knocked the breath from him, though. He quickly put her away from him.

"Nice try, and you're damn tempting, but remember, you're playing against a master of the game. You can't win, baby. Why not make it easy on yourself and give in? It wouldn't be a disgrace to lose."

She pushed out of his embrace and crossed her arms in front of her, taking a deep breath. For a moment he thought her breasts were going to pop out. He wished they'd pop out. He prayed they'd pop out.

Alex was beginning to think maybe the pinkie-swear should be abolished. He and Lisa were adults now. Hell, she was married. If he asked her to pinkie-swear she'd abstain from sex, Lisa would laugh in his face.

"Fine." Kagen broke into his thoughts. "But you have to admit I almost had you. You were *so* ready to have sex with me."

"Was not."

"Were too."

"Think whatever you want, princess, but I wasn't even close to breaking. I just wanted to see how far you'd go."

She glanced at the clock. "I still have the rest of the night and tomorrow." She grinned with self-confidence. "You'll break." She turned on her heel and pranced toward her bedroom.

"Don't count on it," he called after her, watching the sexy sway of her hips. Damn, she'd almost got him that time. It was time he took off the gloves and fought dirty.

He'd love to get dirty with her. He shook his head as he went to the kitchen for a drink. He could think of all kinds of naughty things he'd like to do with her.

That made him wonder again what she'd bought from a store called Guilty Pleasures. The Victoria's Secrets was a gimmie as was the bag from The Candle Shop. But Guilty Pleasures had his imagination running wild.

Whistling softly, he scooped up his package and went to his bedroom. As soon as he was behind closed doors, he removed the liniment and massaged it into his sore arms. Maybe now he could get back to work without aching muscles. The weights had been a really bad idea, he thought as he went back to the living room.

Kagen shut the door of her bedroom and stripped out of her bikini. She knew darn well she'd almost had him down on his knees begging to make love to her. He'd even been prepared. She'd seen the package that could have only come from a drugstore.

Her eyes narrowed thoughtfully. Something stopped him at the last minute, though.

She pulled on underclothes, then a pair of shorts and a tee. Sitting cross-legged on the bed, she opened her package from Guilty Pleasures and bit into a chocolate, cherry-filled truffle. She closed her eyes, moaning with pleasure. Heavenly. The next best thing to a wild night of sex.

There had to be a way to break him. She frowned as she closed the bag and put it back on her dresser.

If she strolled from the bedroom naked, that might get him. But that was against the rules. Well, she had to come up with something pretty fast. *Her* breaking point was close at hand. She didn't even want to think about what he would do next. In fact, maybe she should keep a closer eye on him. Thwart any plans he might have.

Besides, she still wanted to finish accessorizing the living area before she started on the other rooms. She left the bedroom and went to several boxes in the living room that still needed unpacking. As she brought out a box of candleholders, she covertly glanced his way. The screen was still up, but she could see his shadow as he worked at the computer. He looked harmless enough.

She knew better.

She hung a picture over the sofa, then rolled out a braided rug. Her thoughts began to focus on the room. Soon she had it just the way she wanted. A glance at the clock told her she hadn't thought about sex in a whole hour.

"Lisa will love this," Alex said as he stood beside the screen.

Startled, she jumped. Okay, she hadn't thought about sex in, she looked back at the clock, fifty-nine minutes. That was almost an hour.

Still, she couldn't stop the thrill of pleasure that rippled down her spine at his comment. "I hope she will."

He ambled to the sofa and picked up a chenille throw, fingering the material. "This is nice . . . soft."

"Are you trying to seduce me?"

He grinned, and her heart somersaulted. "You want me to?"

She raised her chin. "Not if you won't follow through."

"I'd lose the bet and break my promise to Lisa."

"Some promises are made to be broken."

"You want to eat a bite?" He switched topics. "I mean, get out of the apartment for a while?"

Did he think it would be safer for him? More likely he was up to something. She'd play along because she was hungry. Besides, she'd packed a killer dress. Might as well inflict a little torture while she was at it. "Sure. Just let me change."

An hour later Kagen opened her door. She could tell by the expression on Alex's face as she strolled into the living room he liked what he saw.

The black, sequined dress she wore clung to every curve, flaring just before the hem reached her knees. She'd put her hair up, letting a few curls caress her shoulders.

She watched as his gaze made a downward trek. Past the very low-cut vee, down to legs encased in black stockings, and her feet in three-inch strappy sandals.

"You're ravishing," he told her.

She relaxed, wondering why she was suddenly nervous. "You look pretty good yourself."

She sauntered close enough to catch a whiff of his aftershave. She closed her eyes for a moment, breathing in the musky scent. All she could think about was kissing him, leading him to her bed, and making sweet love all night long. Her brow puckered. Had she caught a whiff of mentholated cream?

"Are you ready?" He took the silk wrap from her arm and held it out for her to slip around her shoulders.

She didn't hesitate as the silk cascaded over her arms. "More than ready."

He chuckled as he guided her toward the front door. "I don't think it's safe for me to be alone with you tonight. A crowded restaurant is a much better choice."

"About to capitulate, are we?" She cast a sidelong glance up at him and fluttered her eyelashes.

Other than a brief smile, he ignored her taunt as he led her out the door, holding her elbow as they walked down the stairs.

"I hope you're not scared of heights."

"Only if I fall."

"Don't worry, I'll catch you if you do."

Her heart fluttered inside her chest. At least she knew how he got his reputation for being a ladies' man.

"I made reservations at The Eiffel Tower Restaurant. Ever been there?"

He opened his car door, and she slid in the passenger seat. "No."

"Lisa and I went there last time I visited. You can't beat it for ambiance, and I think it has the best view of Las Vegas, and the best view of the water show at the Bellagio. Ever seen it?"

"Not up close."

"You're in for a treat, then."

She sighed as she leaned back against the headrest. The night air was inviting. Not too warm, not too cool. Alex's idea had been sound. Maybe she'd needed to get out for a while, too.

The drive was short with each lost in thought. Alex pulled up to the restaurant's valet parking, and they got out. "The only way to reach the restaurant is in the glass elevator. It's eleven stories up."

"The view is beautiful," she said once they were going up in the elevator.

His gaze made a lazy path down her body before returning to her eyes. "It looks great from this angle."

She reached toward him, intending to caress his cheek, but he captured her hand, kissing her palm. Tingles skittered up her arm. The elevator stopped and the doors swished open, preventing her from saying anything else.

The waiter seated them where they would be able to see the water show when it started, then quietly took their order when they were ready.

Alex leaned back in his chair. "What made you decide to become a decorator?"

With only the dim light from the candle on their table, Alex looked quite amiable. But as cute as he was, she sensed he was danger to her. Steve had warned her she couldn't help but get emotionally involved. Was that what she was doing now? Getting emotionally involved?

Kagen had felt more alive over the last few days than she had in a long time. Not to mention more sexually aware. But was that the same thing as losing her heart?

No, she was safe. This was only a sensual game. Foreplay.

"My stepfather taught me the tricks of the trade." Her tense muscles relaxed as she began telling him how she got started. "He has his own businesses. I couldn't have asked for a better teacher."

"Apparently, what you learned paid off. Lisa tells me you have quite a number of stores. Offices in Paris, London, and several in the United States."

"I've been lucky."

He raised his glass in salute. "I'd say it's more than luck."

Don't get excited just because he paid you a compliment, she told herself. She cleared her throat and reached for her wine.

When she could breathe normally again, she set her glass down and met his gaze across the table. "And you? What's your story? Steve told me you create computer programs. You certainly don't look like a computer nerd to me."

He ran his finger over the rim of his wineglass. "I'm glad you approve of how I look." His eyes twinkled, making it hard for her to concentrate. "I like creating programs, coming up with new ideas and implementing them."

"And the one you're working on now?" He'd changed before her eyes. Become more serious. She could tell his work meant a lot to him.

The food they'd ordered arrived about the same time as the show at the Bellagio began, interrupting their conversation. Talking ceased as they enjoyed just being together. When she didn't think Alex was looking, she glanced his way . . . and liked what she saw.

Six

Alex felt like an ass. This was dirty pool. He'd seen the way Kagen had downed two glasses of wine and was just a little tipsy, but he knew damn well he wouldn't be able to last another day around her if she didn't break.

Lying back against the pillows on his bed, he reached for his cell phone on the bedside table, glancing at the clock as he did. Almost midnight. He'd heard her moving about her bedroom a few minutes ago . . . then silence.

He envisioned what she would wear to bed. Maybe the red teddy she'd mentioned . . . or nothing at all. He forced himself to stop thinking about how she'd look lying in bed with only a wisp of silky sheet across her hips, and took a deep, very deep breath before calling the apartment.

It rang once, twice . . .

Pick up the phone, Kagen.

"Hello?" Kagen sounded confused. Apparently wondering why anyone would be calling this late at night.

"I just wanted to tell you good night," he said in what he hoped was a sexy drawl.

"You already did." She chuckled.

He took a deep breath. *Okay, here goes.* "But did I tell you how much I liked the way you'd fixed your hair tonight?

I envied the curls caressing your neck. I wanted to be the one touching you. Kissing you there."

Her indrawn breath came across the line. Without giving her a chance to realize what he was doing, Alex continued in his quest to break her.

"And I liked what you wore tonight. The creamy expanse of skin revealed by the deep vee of that black evening gown was sexy as hell. I itched to slip my hand inside and touch your breasts. To push the dress off one shoulder so I could take you in my mouth."

He closed his eyes, imagining just what Kagen would taste like. Probably a little like the erotic perfume she wore—a tropical taste. And a little like the woman she was—sensual.

He could barely draw a decent breath as he continued. "I would've slid the other side off and massaged your other breast, flicking my finger back and forth across the nipple. Would you have liked that?"

"Yes," she moaned. "Oh, God, yes."

"I would've unzipped the dress and let it fall to the floor. Were you wearing panties?"

"Yes," she croaked.

"What did they look like?"

"Black . . . lacy."

"A thong?"

"No."

"You had on black hose. What held them in place?"

"Garters. Black ones."

"I would've left them on, along with the heels you wore. Picture yourself standing in front of me naked, wearing just your panties, hose, and heels. How does it make you feel to know I'm looking at you? That your breasts are bare?"

"Hot. It makes me hot."

"I'd kneel in front of you and very slowly peel your black, silky panties down those incredibly long legs of yours until the only thing you had on were the black stockings and heels.

I'd lean closer to you, wanting to take your sex in my mouth. Would it bother you if I licked and nibbled you?"

"No. Please, you're killing me, Alex."

"You can stop the torture. Say the word and we won't have to cross each other's paths for the rest of the week. Just say the word, baby."

"Fuck you, Alex."

There was a distinct click. That hadn't been the word he wanted her to utter. Not only that, he had a killer hard-on, and if he didn't do something fast, he'd be the one who broke first. Phone sex. Now that had been a brilliant idea. He wanted her more than ever.

As he slipped on his sweats he heard her bedroom door open, close, then another door open and close. He left his room and hurried past the bathroom. Water pinged against the shower curtain.

His plan had at least worked. Kagen was probably standing beneath a cold spray of water. Now, if he could only jog away his boner. Or at least he hoped running would get rid of it. One thing he could say, after this week he should at least be healthy.

Kagen stuck her tongue out at the screen. Alex was on the other side and couldn't see her childish gesture, but it still made her feel a little vindicated. What he'd done last night was downright cruel. She'd come so close to having an orgasm listening to his husky words. Someday she'd make him pay.

Shaking off her ire, she stepped away from the window and admired the drapes. At least something was turning out well. The decorating was coming right along.

The drapery colors were perfect. The bold maroon and deep green stripes brought out touches of reds and greens in the room while the tea-stained background enhanced the earthy tones of the room.

The living room was finished.

She'd start on the master suite next. The room Alex was using. She should wallpaper it with naked pictures of herself. That wouldn't be cheating . . . exactly.

Who was she kidding? Alex was stronger willed than she'd first thought. He'd never break his promise to Lisa. Besides, she only had a little time left. She'd lost.

Gathering her supplies, she took them to her room. She needed to do something restful. Maybe a hot shower since obviously a cold one wasn't doing the trick. All she'd accomplished was making her nipples harder and more tender. It hadn't cooled her ardor one bit.

She could apply a soothing face mask, light her candles, slip into her new Victoria's Secrets lingerie . . . and read. What was her life coming to?

Thirty minutes later, after a hot shower and a heat-producing face mask, she did feel better. So maybe sex wasn't everything. She donned her white terry cloth robe and stepped from the bathroom, coming face-to-face with Alex. She stuck her nose in the air and sashayed to her room as he went to his.

Just keep telling yourself you don't want to have sex with Alex. Get him out of your system.

She might go out on the town by herself tonight. See the sights of the city that never slept. Might as well since she certainly hadn't been getting any restful slumber.

Damn, she really hated losing, though.

She pulled on the peach-colored thong and push-up bra and stared at herself in the dresser mirror. "You have no idea what you're giving up." She sighed and shook her head.

His loss. She uncurled the cord of her electric razor and plugged it in. It just wasn't fair. This should've been an easy bet to win. But what else was she supposed to do? No getting naked . . . no touching.

But it had felt as if he'd touched her last night. His words had explored her body, making it tingle with awareness. Her eyes closed, and for a moment she relived his phone seduction.

With a shuddering sigh, she reined her thoughts in and sat on the side of the bed. Not fair at all. She flipped the switch and began running the electric razor up and down her leg. Sheesh, even the whirring of the damn razor reminded her of a . . . Her hand stilled. A slow grin spread across her face. It sounded like a vibrator.

Her eyes narrowed as she glanced toward Alex's room as if she could see through the walls. *It's not over yet.*

If he thought she was in the throes of passion, pleasuring herself with a vibrator, would it send *him* over the edge?

What did she have to lose?

She had to make some other noise, though. The vibrator alone wouldn't do it. She closed her eyes and wiggled her bottom into a more comfortable position on the bed.

"Ummmm, ahhhh, ohhhh." She frowned. She sounded like a dying goat. This wasn't going to work. . . . Her gaze landed on her Guilty Pleasures sack. The ceiling opened, and a stream of bright light shone down. Who would've ever thought chocolate could be her savior?

Alex had tried to pretend he didn't notice Kagen or the icy glare she flung in his direction when she stepped from the bathroom. He continued down the hall trying not to breathe in the fresh peach scent that clung to her. Once inside his room, he closed the door and leaned against it. He expelled a deep breath.

How could a woman look so sexy in a white terry cloth robe? The damn thing had been baggy! He was losing it. That's all there was to it.

He pushed away from the door and went to his briefcase in the corner. As soon as he retrieved his disk he'd bury himself behind the screen until the forty-eight hours was up. It was the only way to save his sanity.

He opened the door and walked down the hall, slowing as he neared Kagen's room. Her voice floated to him from the other side of her door.

"Oh, this is good," she moaned. "This is so . . . damn . . . good."

He stumbled to a stop. Was that a motor whirring? A vibrator? Was that what had been in the Guilty Pleasures bag?

"Oh, God, I've got to have more. Oh, yes . . . yes."

Sweat beaded his upper lip. His dick swelled to a full-fledged boner. He didn't want her turning to a vibrator when he was right here.

No, he couldn't do it. He had to think about his meeting . . . his work . . . the promise he'd made to Lisa.

You didn't spit. It doesn't count if you don't spit.

Focus! He squinched his eyes shut.

A vision filled his mind of Kagen lying spread-eagled, completely naked on the bed. She'd touch herself, squeezing her tits with one hand while she slid the vibrator in and out with the other. In and out. In and out.

He braced himself against the wall. *Go to your bedroom and close the door!* His feet wouldn't budge. It was as if he wore concrete boots.

"I want more," she whimpered from the other side. "More."

She was mentally killing him. Would he even be enough to satisfy her needs? He glanced down. He could do it.

"Oh, God, this is sooo . . . good!"

He slammed her door open and stepped purposefully inside. "I'm here for you, Kagen."

She jumped off the bed. A smear of chocolate ran from her lips to the middle of her cheek.

He could only stare at the vision in front of him. Wearing only a very brief, lacy thong that didn't even begin to hide the thatch of dark curls between her legs, and a matching bra that threatened to spill her breasts any second—if he were so lucky.

Candles flickered on the dresser and the bedside table. And on the bed was an electric shaver still whirring away.

Not a vibrator. The Guilty Pleasures sack had toppled over when she stood, and a candy rolled out.

"I'm sorry. I thought . . ." He couldn't stop glancing toward the damn electric razor.

"What?" She followed his line of vision. "Did you think I was having fun without you?" she purred, slowly sucking the chocolate off each of her fingers. He could easily imagine her mouth fitting somewhere else.

She was doing it again . . . trying to make him break first. And she'd nearly succeeded.

Damn it, how could he have been so stupid? "I apologize for interrupting you." He started to back out, but she sauntered forward, quite unembarrassed by her state of dress or, as it were, undress.

"Not so fast."

"I need to get back to work," he mumbled, but he couldn't take his eyes off her. *Remember your promise to . . . to . . . damn, what was his sister's name?*

She shook her head. "Give it up, Alex. You want me."

He tried to leave. He just couldn't get the message from his brain to his feet. She moved in closer for the kill. He drew in a sharp breath. The aroma from the burning candles tickled his senses. He stumbled back. She stepped forward, running her tongue over her lips.

She took his hands and brought them around behind her, planting each one on a bare ass cheek. "Don't you want to have sex with me?"

He struggled to breathe. Damn, her ass felt good. Soft and firm at the same time.

And he really thought the lack of spit would hold up in any court of law as not being a binding agreement.

Seven

If this didn't work, Kagen would give up for good. But from the look in his eyes, and the bulge in his pants, she didn't think he would be able to turn away this time.

"Oh, hell," he mumbled, and lowered his mouth to hers.

Ah, the sweet taste of success. His mouth covered hers in a scorching kiss that sent a burst of fire all the way to her toes and back up where it settled between her legs. Warmth swirled around her, enveloping her in sensuous pleasure.

He moved his mouth to the lobe of her ear and lightly bit, then soothed with a flick of his tongue that sent tingles of pleasure sweeping over her.

"You taste like chocolate—and you're a temptress. Do you know what you've put me through?"

She moaned and closed her eyes. "Like last night wasn't meant to break *me?*"

"Sorry. But you have your revenge." He knelt in front of her. His breath tickling the curls between her legs. "I'm groveling at your feet."

She laughed outright. "No, you're staring."

"That, too." He flicked the lacy triangle with his tongue. "And tasting."

She sucked in a deep breath and grabbed his head to

steady herself as flames shot through her. Closing her eyes tight, she savored the feel of his wet tongue against her most sensitive area.

"Does it bother you that I'm tasting?"

Her breath whooshed out. "On the contrary, I'd rather you not stop."

He ran his tongue up and down the peach-colored lace. His hands cupped her buttocks, drawing her nearer as he nibbled, scraping his teeth across her. His tongue snaked inside the lacy thong, touching . . . licking.

"I can't stand . . ."

"Do you want me to stop?" he asked.

"No, not that. I can't stand anymore. I mean, I'm going to fall over if I don't lie down, and no, I don't want you to stop."

He stood. A whimper escaped at the loss of his tongue against her sex.

"Don't worry. I don't want to stop tasting. But you've pranced around this apartment in sexy clothes until I thought I'd go insane. You owe me." His gaze skimmed over her. "I want to see what's under the wrapping."

And she was happy to oblige. She reached behind for the hook to her bra, but he stayed her hands.

"I like to unwrap my own presents." He turned her around and quickly undid the clasp. "I've dreamt about what you would look like completely naked, lying on the bed, your legs open so I'd be able to see every delicious inch."

He turned her back around, slipping first one strap off her shoulder, then the other. The bra slipped to the floor.

"Nice." He sucked in a mouthful of air and cupped her breasts, rubbing his thumbs across the tender nubs.

She groaned and arched toward him.

He slid his hand downward and slipped two fingers inside her panties, rubbing against her clit. She caught her breath and grabbed his arms to steady herself. She could easily get used to his caressing fingers.

Just before she could experience sweet release from the building tension, he pulled his fingers away. She didn't have time to protest because he began massaging her breasts again, lightly tugging on her nipples. A new pleasure began to build inside her.

When her knees began to buckle, he guided her to the bed and helped her lie down. With her legs dangling off the sides, he pulled her panties off and knelt down. "Now open up to me."

A flutter of indecision raced through her. She wasn't quite sure she wanted to be that exposed. It had been different with the little bit of pink lace covering her.

He nudged her thigh. "I want to see you. I want to taste every inch. I want to run my tongue up and down your clit."

A shudder of excitement swept through her.

He spread her lips open and lightly ran his finger over her. "You're so lovely. Open up for me."

She opened her legs and heard his indrawn breath just before his mouth covered her, sucking, tugging, and pulling on the flesh. She cried out as her hips rose off the bed.

"Do you like that, Kagen?"

"Yes," she cried out. "Ahh, it feels ... so ... good."

"Only good?"

"Great ... fantastic ... *just don't stop.*"

He chuckled and reached a finger toward her. "Maybe I can make it better. Take my finger in your mouth."

"I'd rather suck on something else," she managed to say, but obediently opened her mouth.

"Oh, I plan to let you, but I'm not through with *you* yet."

She dutifully suckled his finger. He groaned.

He tugged his finger away and nudged her legs open farther. "Ah, sweet," he breathed, and inserted his wet finger inside her. "How about this. Do you like this?" Slowly, he moved his finger inside ... then out. Her breath came in little gasps as he moved faster. He lowered his mouth to her once more and began licking while his finger kept up a steady pace.

"Come for me, baby," he murmured against her.

She didn't disappoint him as spasms trembled down her body and exploded into an orgasm. She cried out, her body going limp. This was what she'd been waiting for all her life. As the spasms continued to rock through her she vaguely saw Alex strip. She wanted to watch, but she was still caught up in the sensations sweeping over her. There would be time enough later. She had no doubt about that.

He lay beside her on the bed and ran his hand lightly over her sweaty body before cupping one breast and rubbing the pad of his thumb over her nipple. "I loved watching your face when you came."

"I'm glad I pleased you. I think I can do better than an expression, though."

She drew in a shaky breath, reached down, and circled his hard penis. He sucked in a deep breath as she ran her hand over the tip, enjoying the smooth, slick feel. Renewed energy rushed through her. She nudged him onto his back, wanting to give him as much pleasure as he'd given her.

She ran her tongue over his chest, flicking across each nipple, and moving her head lower, swirling her tongue over the end of his shaft before taking him into her mouth.

He groaned and arched his hips. "You don't know how many times I've dreamt of your mouth on me like this."

As had she. He tasted wonderful. Smooth and satiny. She couldn't get enough.

"No more or I'll explode," he finally groaned.

"Tit for tat." She grinned, liking the fact that she was in control.

He scooped under her arms and slid her slick body up his. "I want to be inside you. I'll have to get something out of my room first, though."

From her position on top of him she could reach her dresser if she stretched. "I've got you covered."

"In more ways than one."

She chuckled and brought out a handful of foil packets. "Ribbed or smooth."

"It won't matter if we don't hurry." His pained expression said it all.

"Then by all means, let's not dally." There would be a lot more time to dally around later. She glanced down. "Extra large." She ripped one of the packets open.

Exactly how did one do this? She'd never actually put a condom on a man before. No time like the present. Besides, how hard could it be? She glanced down at him and smiled. Nice and hard.

She rather enjoyed sliding the rubbery material over his erection. And from the look on Alex's face, he didn't mind her touching him.

Before she had any time at all to admire her handiwork, he'd flipped her onto her back and prodded her legs open, slipping inside. She didn't even get a chance to explain she wasn't through checking him out. When he pushed deeper, all reasonable thoughts departed.

He filled her. Her body closed snugly around him. She brought her legs up and wrapped them around his waist. Her inner muscles clenched and unclenched.

"You're tight," he moaned with pleasure.

She arched toward him. "You're big."

Kagen thought she heard him chuckle; she wasn't sure and didn't really care as he started a friction of heat inside her with each thrust. She briefly wondered if this was the way cavemen had discovered how to make fire.

All thoughts ceased to exist as passion gripped her body and she climaxed. Alex jerked and groaned. He eased himself down, making sure his weight wasn't resting on her before rolling onto his side.

The sound of their ragged breathing filled the room. Kagen didn't want this magical spell that had been cast over them to dissipate. She felt too good. All warm and cozy. Alex snuggled her into the crook of his arm, and she felt complete.

"I'm sorry you broke your promise to Lisa," she told him on a yawn.

"Really?"

She thought about it for a moment. "No, it just seemed the thing to say."

She lay back against the pillows, closing her eyes as sweet exhaustion claimed her mind and body. As she drifted into a light sleep her thoughts were on Alex, and she knew this was going to be the best week of her life.

Alex slowly came awake. Kagen had turned over and was snuggled in the crook of his arm, spoon fashion. He reached toward her but drew his hand back at the last minute.

Ah hell, what had they done? What had *he* done? A sharp image of Kagen sucking and licking him filled his mind. Great! Not awake more than a few minutes and she already had him hard and hurting—and she was still sound asleep!

But the cure for his pain was nestled next to him.

Don't even go there. He eased away from her. She moaned softly and rolled to her back.

It wouldn't take much to have her hot and ready for him. His hungry gaze devoured her breasts. Just one touch, one scrape of his fingers across her tender nipples, and they'd harden. His gaze lowered, sweeping past her flat stomach, and stopping at the curls between her legs. Hiding what he'd looked upon earlier, what he'd tasted. What his tongue had explored.

As if sensing his need to see more of her, she shifted her position, one knee crooked, exposing her to his view.

Alex drew in a sharp breath; his hand reached toward her. He pulled back at the last moment. But even though his hand was stayed, he couldn't stop feasting his eyes on her beauty. This was the essence of her being. The heart of the woman she was.

"It's okay to touch," she spoke so softly he thought at first he'd only imagined her words. But when she took his hand and guided it downward, toward the vee of her legs, he knew he hadn't.

He hesitated.

She smiled. "You can't unbreak the promise you made. The damage is done." She sighed. "Do you really think Lisa will care that much?"

He grinned. "No, you're right."

She surprised him by rolling on top of his body and staring down into his face. "Good, then will you shut up and make love to me?" She closed her eyes and arched her back so she had a tighter fit against the lower half of his body. "Umm, that feels good."

Her hands rested on her thighs as she raised up and slid down, impaling her body on his. He watched through slitted eyes. The rise and fall of her breasts, her ragged breathing. He watched it all until his eyes glazed with passion and he lost himself in the moment and everything it had to offer.

She pumped faster and faster. Her hot body closing over his, her muscles contracting and releasing. He grabbed her ass, going with the motion, raising his hips for each thrust. His body exploded in a sensation of hot lights and erotic sounds as he came.

Seconds later, Kagen grabbed her thighs and groaned, then crumpled to his chest. Their ragged breathing filled the room.

Eight

As she lay against Alex's chest, Kagen could hear his heart beating. She liked the steady rat-a-tat-tat blending with her own heartbeat. In fact, everything about the last few hours had been satisfying. She sighed.

"I suppose I need to get back to work. I still have more to do on my program if I want to have it ready in time for my meeting," he interrupted her thoughts.

Satisfying until now, that was. She raised her head and looked at him. "Wham, bam, thank you, ma'am?"

He smiled. She decided she liked the way his lips curved upward. Humor went all the way to his eyes and twinkled in the corners.

"I don't think the last hour or so could be called a quickie," he informed her.

"No, you're right. Definitely a longie." She folded her hands and rested her chin on them, averting her eyes away from his face. "You can't very well go back to the computer before you shower."

"Are you saying I smell?"

"No, just that you'd be uncomfortable. I mean, all sweat-dried and icky feeling."

"And what exactly are you suggesting?"

She lightly drew circles on his chest with her finger. "Just that we might save water by bathing together. Steve and Lisa's tub is awfully large . . . and a whirlpool. It'd be a shame if we didn't try it out at least once."

It wasn't hard for her to imagine the two of them naked in a tub filled with bubbles. She'd scrub his back . . . he'd scrub hers. *Admit it, you're fascinated with the man and want the moment to last.* But it was just a fascination. She wasn't getting emotionally involved. She wouldn't let herself.

"Steve and Lisa might care if they knew exactly what we'd do in their bathtub," Alex said.

Her eyes met his. "I won't tell if you won't."

"Deal."

She liked the devilish quirk almost as much as his sweet smile. No, maybe better. It made her wonder just what he was thinking.

"I'll start the water." She scooted off him, and the bed. She could feel his intense gaze as she made her way across the room. Good. She wanted him to look.

At the doorway, she turned, giving him a full frontal view. His gaze slowly slid down her body. She liked the compliment his eyes paid her. It was better than any words.

She slipped out the door, chuckling when she heard his frustrated groan. Once inside the large bathroom, she turned the faucets on, adding a small amount of fragrant bubble bath. As water poured into the tub, the rich scent of vanilla began filling the room. Her body tingled with the thought of what the two of them could do. It didn't matter they'd already enjoyed the last couple of hours or so exploring each other's body. She wanted him again.

Now to finish setting the mood. She retraced her steps and went back to the bedroom, frowning when she saw Alex wasn't in the bed.

What if he'd decided not to join her in the bathtub after all?

She was still frowning when she walked back into the

bathroom with the candles and relit them. Before she could dwell on the *what if*s, Alex stepped into the room balancing a tray of food with one hand and holding two glasses and a bottle of beer in the other.

"I thought we could have a bathtub picnic. No wine, though. We'll have to settle for beer." He smiled. "You don't mind that I swiped some of your chocolate, do you? I have a terrible sweet tooth."

A man after her heart. She sauntered over to him and took the beer and glasses. "I love a man with good taste." And he tasted very good. She set the glasses and bottle on a small table she pulled near the tub. He put the tray beside it, stole a bon-bon, and popped it into his mouth.

"You have excellent taste in chocolate."

"Umm . . . remind me to show you what I can do with a bottle of chocolate syrup."

He sucked in a deep breath. "I think I'll hold you to that."

She turned off the water, while he climbed in on the opposite end of the faucets. She joined him, snuggling comfortably against his chest, white bubbles surrounding them.

"Tell me some more about your computer program," she asked as he poured half the beer into a glass and handed it to her. She wanted to know more about him. Good idea, since they'd already known each other quite intimately.

If someone had told her last week she'd be sitting naked in a tub with a man she barely knew, she would've laughed herself silly. But here she was—and it seemed so damn right. She listened as Alex began to talk.

"It's a new software program. I'm meeting with two possible investors tomorrow. If I can convince them to back me with the financial end, then I'll have the money to market the program." He paused. "I'm probably boring you."

She took a sip of her beer. "On the contrary, I'm very interested. Tell me more." She'd heard the passion in his voice and knew this meant a lot to him.

He lightly stroked her breast. He probably wasn't even

aware he touched her, but she was. She focused her thoughts and tried to pay attention to what he was telling her.

"It's sort of like a virtual reality program."

She cleared her mind of her sexual fantasies and concentrated on the conversation. "Hasn't that been done before?"

"Sort of, but not like this. Other people have marketed a 3D diagram of a room. This is actually a hologram."

"I'm confused."

His hand stilled. "Okay, imagine a house contractor and a buyer. If the contractor could project the interior as a hologram, the buyer would be able to stand in the middle of each room and see it as a finished project. They could change the dimensions, the type of flooring, or tile with the click of a button. Do you realize how much money the buyer would save? Not to mention the contractor a lot of future headaches. The possibilities are endless."

Suddenly what he said became very interesting. Her eyes narrowed. "How much would a program like this cost?"

"More money than I have. But hey, that's why I'm meeting with the investors tomorrow. I'll show it to you later if you still want to see it." He cleared his throat and refilled her glass. "How do you know Steve?"

"Steve and I lived next door to each other all through junior high and most of high school."

"It must've been some friendship to have stayed in touch all these years."

She smiled. "It was. At least until my mother remarried and we moved away."

"I bet it was tough losing your best friend and getting a stepfather all at the same time."

"Tony's cool, so I couldn't resent him for long. He bought me and Steve computers so we could e-mail each other every day."

"Generous of him."

"But Tony's more than that. He loves Mom a lot. My real

dad walked out on us right after I was born. She didn't trust any man after that. Tony wouldn't take no for an answer, though. It was sweet watching him chase her."

"And you and Steve. I mean, you weren't romantically involved?"

"Only if you count we shared our very first kiss." She laughed. "I think we both felt the same. It was like kissing a sibling. We decided we liked being friends instead."

"Good. I'd hate to be jealous of my new brother-in-law." He set his glass on the table and cupped her breasts, rubbing his thumbs across her nipples. He started a sweet ache deep inside her. She was so caught up in the sensations that she didn't realize her glass tilted until it was too late and she'd dumped the contents on her chest. She gasped as the cold liquid hit her warm skin.

"A shame to waste beer." He pulled her around until she faced him, her legs crossing over his. He kissed each breast, lapping up the brew. She arched her back, her hands grasping his shoulders.

He drew her bottom nearer to his erection, rubbing her body against his. She closed her eyes, savoring the brush of him against her.

"Open your mouth."

She dutifully obeyed.

"Bite."

She did. A chocolate truffle. God, it was good. Cherry-filled. Sex and chocolate. It didn't get any better than this.

He brought her closer, nibbling her neck, moving toward her mouth until his covered hers. His tongue sought and captured. He tasted like chocolate and heat . . . and he tasted like Alex. It was a better than good combination.

Jets suddenly came alive when he pushed a button. Rushing water came toward her in several different directions. He raised her hips slightly, and the water shot between her legs, massaging and tickling her sex.

She moaned. "Remind me to get one of these whirlpool tubs." It had a vibrating intensity that was sexually stimulating.

"Only if you share it with me."

"Deal."

He pulled a condom on as the bubbles rose around them. She slid over him, taking him inside her body. The friction of his hips and the water brought her to a quick orgasm. He apparently enjoyed it, too, because he came seconds later. When their gazes met, they both smiled. The smiles soon turned to laughter. There were bubbles everywhere.

He turned off the jets. "Hungry?"

"I never realized just how starved I was."

He smiled, and again the corners of his eyes twinkled. They fed each other rolled-up slices of ham and chicken, and as the bubbles dissipated, she wondered if this moment might last forever.

Nine

"Help you do what?" Kagen knew she was looking at Alex as though he was crazy, but she couldn't help herself. Why would she move the furniture when she finally had it the way she wanted?

"You're the one who said you were interested in knowing more about my program. To do it justice I'll need open space."

Darn, she didn't want to move the furniture. But he was right, she wanted to see his program. "Okay, let's do it."

When all the furniture had been pushed to the side, Alex went to the computer and inserted a disk. After adjusting a video camera, he glanced her way.

"Ready?"

She nodded.

He hit a key on the computer, and his sister's living room became a kitchen. It was unbelievable. Her gaze slowly scanned the room. There were pine cabinets, all the appliances, and even though she knew she was standing on carpet, when she looked down what she saw was a hardwood floor. "Amazing," she muttered and stepped forward.

"Watch out for the island," Alex warned.

"What island?"

His fingers clicked open a box. He scrolled down and hit

enter. Seconds later an island appeared right in front of her, complete with pots and pans hanging above it. She reached out to touch the green marble counter, but her hand went right through it. Laughter spilled from her. "Ghost cabinets."

He smiled. "You could say that."

"This is fantastic."

"You really think so?"

"Yes . . . no, better than fantastic. I can't believe someone hasn't snatched this up and run with it."

"I haven't really marketed it. Instead, I'm looking for investors. I'm trying to keep it out of the hands of a major company so I don't lose control of my product." He suddenly grinned. "So, you really like it?"

"Yes, I do. A lot. Except your color choices aren't the best. You're in a time warp. No one has avocado green appliances anymore."

"Childhood memory." He grinned a little sheepishly and shrugged. "Besides, we all can't be interior decorators. I can easily change the color, though." He brought up another box, scrolled down, and hit enter. The green appliances became white. "Better."

"Better. But what if I don't like the style of the cabinets or the countertop?"

"That's the beauty of this program. If you were the buyer and I were the contractor, we could look at each room. Change the dimensions, the colors, the style of cabinets *before* construction . . . All I have to do is input everything. The possibilities are endless."

"This is great, Alex."

He paused.

"What?" He was leaving something out.

"Well, I've been experimenting in another area as well."

"Show me." The man was a genius. There was no doubt in her mind.

Alex popped out the disk, and the room returned to normal. He dug around inside his briefcase and brought out another disk, but before he inserted it, he looked her way.

"Do you like the ocean?"

"I love it." Why did he want to know? She didn't think he could create a private jet that would whisk them off to the coast. Patience, she told herself.

He put the disk into the slot and began opening and clicking on boxes. When he hit the enter key she was suddenly standing on a sandy beach with waves lapping at her feet.

"Wow. An ocean in the middle of Las Vegas."

"Wait, I'm not through yet."

He clicked open more boxes, and the light faded to black as brilliant stars appeared in the sky. Suddenly there was sound, and she could actually hear the surf pounding against the rocks.

She walked forward, and it even looked as if she was going into deeper waters. "How did . . ."

She froze. A fin came toward her. Shark! She whirled around and ran straight into Alex's arms. His chest rumbled with laughter, and she realized she'd been running from a projected image.

Damn it, the shark looked real. "That wasn't funny."

"Okay, I'll quit laughing." His chest continued to shake.

"You're still laughing."

"Sorry."

"I just bet you are." But she snuggled against his warm body, a smile curving her lips. "How did you do it?"

"I never reveal my secrets." He ran his hand up and down her back. "Ever made love on a sandy beach?" he whispered close to her ear.

Tingles of excitement ran up and down her arms. "No, but I think I'd like to."

"You're like no other woman I've ever met," he said. "And I'm glad you went after what you wanted."

"Why should it be any different for a woman than it is a

man? We have the same needs." She stepped out of his arms. The shark swam around her ankles. "Do you mind getting rid of Jaws, though?" She looked pointedly down at her feet.

"Would you rather have Flipper?"

She lowered her voice to a husky whisper. "What I'd rather have is you naked."

"I think I can oblige." He went to the computer and began opening boxes. The shark disappeared. He scrolled down and clicked again, and the sensuous strains of island music mingled with the ocean's waves.

Kagen laughed lightly and began unbuttoning her top. No man had ever affected all her senses like Alex did right now.

When he turned back around she let her top slide down her arms and drop into the imaginary ocean. As he came toward her he pulled his tee over his head and tossed it to the side.

He was magnificent. Shadows danced across his bare torso in a play of light from the twinkling stars above them. She reached behind her back and unhooked her bra, shrugged her shoulders, and let it drop to the floor.

"You're beautiful," he said.

"I was thinking the same thing about you," she breathed.

He pulled a bottle of oil from the pocket of his sweats and held it up. "I'd hate for you to get sunburned."

"Did you have this planned? And besides, it's nighttime." Her thighs quivered at the thought of him spreading oil over her naked flesh.

"Let's just say I was hoping. You know, even though there's no sun, the breeze could chafe your skin."

His expression reminded her of a little boy before Christmas who wanted to open his present early. But this wasn't a little boy standing in front of her. Alex was all man.

She thought about explaining there was no wind. "You're right. It could blister me." It was much better to pretend.

He flipped the top open and drizzled oil on her shoulders.

The droplets began slowly sliding down her chest, tickling, caressing. She sucked in a deep breath.

"Nice?"

"Ummm . . . Nicer than nice. Your turn."

He shook his head. "I have a better idea."

She was really starting to like his ideas. A lot.

He tugged her close until her nipples grazed his chest. The oil smeared from her body to his. She closed her eyes, lost in the moment of flesh against flesh. But she wanted more.

She slid her hands inside his sweats and pushed them downward while he did the same with her shorts until they were standing naked in the middle of the living room, surrounded by a sandy beach and ocean. It was wonderful, romantic. He'd given her the moon, the stars, and the surf. No man had ever done that.

"You're beautiful in the moonlight," he told her. "Dance with me."

They swayed together with the music drumming in their ears. Two bodies became one. For a while time stood still in this make-believe paradise.

Alex picked the oil up off the floor where he'd let it fall atop his discarded clothes. He drizzled more on her front, then turned her, and did the same to her back. With her bottom snuggled against his erection, he began moving his hands over her. Caressing her breasts, tweaking the nipples. She moaned, leaning her head back against his chest.

His hands continued their downward trek, sliding over her thighs, coming close to her sex but not touching. She moaned, wanting . . . needing him to stroke her, to bring her to the point of release.

"Alex, you're killing me," she moaned.

"More?"

She nodded, even that was difficult.

He lowered her to the carpet and began kissing her breasts. Giving each hardened nipple his attention while his fingers drew circles along her belly, always moving downward. She arched her hips, her body begging for relief as her breath came out in small puffs.

His fingers began to stroke her. The first waves of an orgasm caught her with tidal force, taking her higher and higher until it crested. She caught her breath, riding out the wave of pleasure as sweet release swept over her like the waves surrounding her, but what she felt wasn't imaginary. It was real.

She turned toward him, burying her head against his chest . . . wanting the connection to be complete. As if he sensed her need, he entered her, rolling her onto her back. She wrapped her legs around his waist, drawing him closer still. He rocked against her, slowly at first, and then faster. She met each thrust. He groaned when he reached climax.

As the tide of their passion ebbed, Kagen knew without a doubt she was falling in love. Steve had been right, she'd let herself get emotionally involved.

They fell asleep that night wrapped in each other's arms, but her dreams were filled with Alex looking at her with pity because she was stupid enough to fall in love with him.

When she woke the next morning her head was pounding. Alex was moving quietly about the room. From the dampness of his hair, she could see he'd already taken a shower.

"I didn't mean to wake you." He strolled to the side of the bed and dropped a kiss on top of her head.

She snuggled his pillow and offered a smile, even though she knew what had to be done. "Your meeting?"

He nodded and turned the blow-dryer on.

"Nervous?" she asked when he finished.

His expression turned serious. "Yeah, I've invested most of my money into this program."

She sat up in bed, crossing her feet in front of her. "It's a really good program. They can't help but like it."

He slipped his jacket on and grabbed his briefcase. "I hope you're right. I'll see you this afternoon."

"Bye." Her heart broke when the front door shut. The only thing waiting for him would be her note telling him she'd had a crisis at one of her stores. Nothing major but she'd had to leave. Business. He'd understand.

This was the only way. No tears. No pitying looks. Just a simple goodbye. But if it was so simple, then why did it hurt so blasted much?

Ten

He wasn't ready for the meeting. Alex knew he could've worked a few more hours. Perfected the program a little more. Damn, it was now or never. He straightened his tie and strode purposefully inside the Regents building. The offices of Dunbar and Craig were on the eighteenth floor. Heights were becoming a regular in his life.

Kagen had certainly taken him higher than he'd ever been. He was smiling as he stepped inside the elevator and pushed number eighteen. The ride up was smooth. As smooth as Southern Comfort, as smooth as making love to Kagen. No, not to—with. She'd given as much as she'd taken.

The doors whizzed silently open after the elevator came to a stop.

He blinked twice. Whatever he'd expected, it wasn't this. Not the total chaos that greeted him. People were everywhere—boxing up files and equipment. A harried receptionist tried to answer constantly ringing phones. An older woman hurried past with a cardboard box filled with papers, a silver picture frame, and an ivy with leaves draped over the side of the box.

"Excuse me," he began. "I'm supposed to be meeting with Elaine Dunbar and Warren Craig today at three."

"Oh, dear, Ms. Dunbar has left the country, and no one knows exactly where Mr. Craig went."

An icy chill of dread ran down his spine. "I beg your pardon."

She nodded as tears filled her eyes. "I know. It's just terrible. They filed bankruptcy. It was a shock to us all."

He could feel the color draining from his face. "But they were supposed to look at my computer program," he spoke almost to himself.

"Oh, yes, you must be Mr. Cannedy. I remember you had an appointment with them." She straightened. "I was her secretary." Just as quickly her shoulders slumped. "Now I'm unemployed."

And he was up the creek without a paddle and his canoe was sinking fast. Apparently some of his dismay showed on his face because she looked sympathetic.

"I'm so sorry, young man. I'm sure you'll find someone else to look at your program."

"Yes, I'm sure I will," he mumbled, and went back inside the elevator.

Odd, he thought on the way to the first floor, how one minute you could feel confident and sure your dreams were about to materialize, and within seconds all your hopes were dashed against the wall.

He'd poured all his money into a program that might never see the light of day. Unless he could find someone else interested in his work.

At least there was still one bright light in his life. Kagen would be at the apartment waiting for him. Odd how losing the investors didn't seem so bad. Kagen was right. It was a good program, and he'd be able to find someone else interested in backing it.

Suddenly he was in a hurry to get back to her. There was a lot more he wanted to learn about Kagen.

Time dragged as he waited in traffic. Minutes seemed like hours. When the cars started moving, he noticed a flower shop. A few more minutes wouldn't matter that much, but he had a feeling it would mean a lot to Kagen if he brought her flowers. She seemed to love different scents and colors.

He made a detour and ran inside the flower shop, leaving the motor running.

When he finally arrived at the apartment it seemed as though he'd been gone forever. His pulse raced as he opened the door and rushed inside.

"What has been going on here?" Lisa jumped to her feet and, like an angry storm cloud, strode toward him.

Alex carefully placed the roses and his keys on the table. "What are you doing home?" He looked around the living room. "And where's Kagen?"

Steve came up and put his arm around Lisa's shoulders. "Calm down, sweetie." He looked at Alex. "She got seasick, so we flew home rather than take the boat back."

"You broke your promise." Lisa sniffed, waving a paper under his nose. "Especially after she made the living room so fantastic. How could you?"

He grabbed the paper out of her hand and began to read.

Dear Alex,

I'm so sorry but I have to leave. A minor crisis at one of my stores. I know you'll understand. Hey, we had a great time together. At least this way we won't have any messy goodbyes.

Take care of yourself.

Love,
Kagen

Alex plodded to the sofa and dropped onto the cushion. He stared at the letter, his life tumbling down around him. He pictured Kagen's laugh, the way she'd challenged him with a cockiness he adored. In a few short days, she'd become his whole life.

"You've never broken a promise to me. Why did you have to break this one?"

"I know why." Steve spoke up as if he'd just realized something that left him floored. "He's in love."

"Yeah, right," Lisa said, and laughed without humor.

"No, look at him. That's the face of a man in love. Believe me, I know it well."

Alex ran a hand over his eyes. "A lot of good it will do me. Apparently, the feeling isn't mutual." How could so much go so wrong in one day? No investors *and* no Kagen.

"You really love her?" Lisa sat next to him on the sofa, taking his hand in hers.

He met her eyes. "Yeah, I think I do, but it doesn't matter what we had. She's gone."

"Not exactly," Steve said as he returned from the direction of the kitchen. Alex hadn't even been aware when he'd left the room. "I just got off the phone with the airline. Her plane hasn't left yet. If you hurry, you can catch her."

Alex's dismal mood didn't brighten. "You read the letter. It's over."

"But I also know Kagen. She's never run from a relationship. She always tried to make it work. I think she might care for you."

"And if you're wrong?"

"You won't know unless you go after her."

Lisa nudged his arm. "Go. Don't let her get away."

What if he did mean something to her? He certainly had strong feelings for her.

He came to a quick decision and jumped to his feet. As he scooped up his keys, he called over his shoulder, "I'll call you later."

Kagen shifted in the seat she'd taken next to the window in the airport bar. She sipped her wine as she counted down the minutes before she would enter the restricted area of the terminal. She'd much rather stay here and get totally inebriated.

If she was doing the right thing, then why did she have this horrible sinking feeling in the pit of her stomach? All she could think about was Alex. Maybe if she went back to the apartment and told him she'd like to explore the relationship a little more just to see if maybe there was something there, he would. . . . Who was she trying to fool?

She'd seduced *him*. She'd wanted a burn-up-the-sheets weekend of pleasure. But he'd given her more than that. He'd made her laugh, he'd made her determined to win their silly little bet, he'd made her smile . . . he'd made her fall in love. Ah jeez, she'd fallen in love with the guy.

Now it was over. At least he wouldn't see her tears. She sniffed. Everyone else in the blasted airport would, but not Alex. Never Alex. She sniffed again and began digging around in her purse for a tissue.

She finally found a small package in the very bottom. She tore it open and yanked one out. As she wiped her eyes, her vision cleared.

She was losing her mind; either that, or Alex was in the airport. Why would Alex be walking purposefully toward her terminal? Maybe the man only resembled Alex. She could be suffering post-relationship trauma syndrome or something. But the closer he got to the bar, the more positive she became.

He happened to glance her way. His jaw set in a determined line as he changed direction and walked toward her.

What was he doing here? She jerked to her feet, smoothing her hands down the sides of her slacks. Oh, Lord, her nose was probably red from crying, and she hadn't even bothered with make-up before she'd left. This would make a great lasting impression.

"Where do you think you're going?" he asked, stopping in front of her.

"Didn't you get my note?" She'd propped it against the counter in plain sight.

"Yeah, and I read the part about you leaving. Now I want to know why. The real reason. Not some lame excuse about problems at one of your stores."

She felt like a slowly deflating tire. "What's a few days here or there?"

"You didn't finish decorating the apartment."

"I'm going to send one of my assistants to finish the job. You won't have any problems with him like you did with me. You'll be able to work on your computer program whenever you like."

"The deal fell through."

Oh, no, he must be devastated. She knew what getting his program off the ground meant to him. "I'm so sorry."

"It doesn't matter. What matters is that you don't end what we have together."

She closed her eyes as a rush of joy swept over her. He didn't want it to end. At the same time a speck of doubt crept up, dampening her elation. Was he only looking for another investor? She didn't want to listen to the little devil perched on her shoulder, but she'd been burned too many times in the past.

She made a quick decision, opened her eyes, and took a deep breath. "I want to invest in your program."

His brow furrowed. "What? I thought we were talking about us?"

"We are, but first I want to offer you a business proposition. I like your program. It could easily be incorporated into my interior design company *and* used with house contractors. Do we have a deal?"

He took a step away from her. "Is that why you think I came looking for you? Do you think I did it so you'd invest in my program?"

"Please," she pleaded. "It's a good deal. I'll offer what you were planning on getting from the other investors with the knowledge I can use it in my business, too." She stuck her hand out. "My stepfather taught me a handshake was as good as a signed document. Shake my hand and we'll seal the deal."

He hesitated before taking her hand in a firm grip and shaking it.

Now she had to let him go.

"You're free. You can pursue any woman you want. I'll keep my end of the bargain." Her smile wavered. "My lawyers will draw up all the necessary documents. I'll have some of my people meet with you to go over exactly how you can incorporate the program into my home designs."

"You'll let me go? Just like that. I can date any woman I want and you won't back out of the deal?"

She nodded, not really trusting her voice.

"Great. I know just the woman. She's vibrant, beautiful, sexy, puzzling at times, confusing, wild in bed, but a little touched in the head if she thinks I could ever love anyone other than her." He took her in his arms, lowering his mouth to hers.

He loved her! Alex had said he loved her. She hadn't misunderstood. He'd also said she was touched in the head, too. It didn't matter.

The kiss ended, and he snuggled her close. "Please don't ever leave me. When you left you took my world, you took my heart, you took my reason for living."

"I love you so much," she whispered as the airport disappeared, along with the people, and once more she got lost in his kiss.

Please turn the page for an
exciting preview of
TURN LEFT AT SANITY
by Nancy Warren.

A February 2005 release from Brava.

"Do you remember George Murdoch?" asked Aunt Lydia around a mouthful of cucumber sandwich. "He was a fine, fine man." At seventy-five, Aunt Lydia was an improbable redhead with a tendency to live in the past.

The fine-boned woman on the blue velvet settee, whose hair was white and float-away delicate, nodded. "He was hung."

"Really, dear? I thought they'd done away with capital punishment in Idaho," said Betsy Carmichael, who'd come in her Sunday best to take tea.

"More tea, ladies?" Emmylou walked amongst them with the heavy silver tea pot. Afternoon tea at the Shady Lady bed and breakfast in Beaverton, Idaho, was a tradition Emmylou had started a year or so ago when she realized she was going to need a lot more business if she was going to make a go of running a B&B in a town where tourism was zip and the local industries were . . . unconventional.

After filling the bone china teacups she brought out every Sunday, she passed around the cucumber sandwiches and the thin slices of lemon cake she'd baked from a recipe in a ten-year-old issue of *Gourmet* magazine. She didn't figure in a house that was a hundred and fifty years old, its full-time residents not much younger, that anyone would care if she served a decade old recipe. There were days she thought no one would notice if she served decade old cake.

She had to admit that afternoon tea wasn't a roaring success. No one but the aunts who lived at the Shady Lady and their friends, who were too poor to pay, ever showed up, but it had become such a Sunday afternoon ritual that Emmylou kept it up anyway. It gave them something to do, a chance to dress up in their finery, and she suspected they enjoyed the chance to reminisce about their good old days.

Emmylou knew all the stories as well as though she'd been there when the Shady Lady had been upgraded from boom town brothel to become a vital part of the innovative Dr. Emmet Beaver's practice for healthful living both mental and physical, and the ladies gathered in the sitting room had been Intimate Healers.

Now they were old ladies and Emmylou, who'd grown up here, was their collective granddaughter since her beloved gran had passed on.

The sound of the doorbell shocked the assembled company of women into silence. The doorbell never rang. Anyone who lived in Beaverton would walk on in; the door was never locked. If they wanted afternoon tea, they knew to walk straight into the parlor.

"Could it be a guest?" Lydia wondered out loud, looking hopeful.

At the words, Olive sat straighter and rearranged the folds of her red silk dress to best advantage. Since she was self-conscious about her varicose veins, she crossed her legs and tucked them against the brocade sofa.

"I'll go and check," Emmylou said. She'd tried over and over to explain to Lydia that "guest" had a different connotation now that the Shady Lady was a B&B than it had forty years ago.

She didn't have any bookings coming in today. Heck, she didn't have any bookings all month—it wasn't hard to keep track. Probably, Geraldine Mullet had been watching *Gone with the Wind* again and was here to warn them all that the Yankees were at the door ready to burn their barns and commandeer their plantation houses. When she was bound and determined to save Tara, Geraldine wasn't bad company. It was when she suggested burning the place themselves so those damned Yankees couldn't get their grubby hands on it that Emmylou had to draw on all her tact.

Only when Emmylou emerged from the parlor to the entrance foyer, it wasn't Geraldine standing there looking like Vivien Leigh might look today if she were still alive.

In her hall was a man she'd never set eyes on before.

A gorgeous man.

He was tall, with black hair that would have been completely straight but for the errant cowlick above his left eyebrow. His eyes were pewter gray, or maybe steel. He had the kind of face that made her remember that the heavy silver tea pot she still held was sterling, and wish she'd hidden it before blundering out here.

If it had been civil war times, he wouldn't have been gambling ne'er do well Clark Gable, he'd have been a union officer here to take what he could get, whatever her opinions on the matter. He didn't look to be a charmer or a gambler, this one, he looked like a hard-eyed predator.

She swallowed and said, "Can I help you?"

He turned those eyes on her and she felt a prickle of sensation climb her neck. Fear? Curiosity? She couldn't name it, but the feeling left her feeling uneasy and a little breathless.

"Yes. I understand this is the only hotel in town." His voice was crisp and completely unaccented, as though any kind of twang or lilt would be a waste of his precious time. No pleasantries, either, she noted, though his eyes gave her a very thorough once over while she stood there staring.

"That's right," she said, feeling that business was business and no matter how uncomfortable he made her feel, she was going to be nice to him. He was obviously a guy with enough money for the best clothes, like the casual but no-doubt expensive charcoal slacks and black turtle neck sweater. His briefcase looked designed by Nasa; he gave off the impression of having finished a business meeting in Manhattan and hopped on his Lear jet to get here. Clearly the Lear pilot had no sense of direction or he'd been drinking on the job, because Mr. Corporate had taken a wrong turn somewhere.

But, she reminded herself once again, business was business and he didn't look as though he'd have any trouble paying his bill. Although, when you lived in a town like Beaverton you didn't give much credence to appearances.

"I can wait, if you're in the middle of something," he said, polite but cool, motioning to the silver pot.

"Oh, no, that's all right," she said, carefully setting the pot on a marble-topped vanity that also held a bouquet of deep pink peonies in a crystal vase, their thin stems struggling to hold the overblown glory of the blooms.

She stepped behind the ornate reception desk that was built into the foyer and pulled out the leather-bound registration book she'd found in an antique shop. Flipping to a fresh page, she passed it, and a vintage fountain pen, to her new guest.

Aunt Olive had tried to talk her into a computerized reservation system, but she liked the simple, old-fashioned book. It fit with the period of the Shady Lady and was well able to handle the few paying guests they received. It was also a heck of a lot cheaper, and sadly, money was a factor in every decision these days.

She watched as the newest guest wrote his name in a bold but perfectly legible scrawl. Like his speaking voice, his penmanship displayed no extra flourishes, no wasted time, no wasted ink. No nonsense.

When he was done, she read over his entry. Joe Montcrief was his name, and she was pleased to find she'd guessed correctly. His address was in Manhattan.

"And how long will you be staying with us, Mr. Montcrief?" she asked in her best B&B proprietor's tone.

"It's Joe," he said. She got the impression that it wasn't informality that made him tell her that, more that he didn't want the extra time wasted with all those syllables. He'd even knocked the "seph" from the Joseph. He should be glad his parents hadn't christened him Mortimer, or Horatio. "I'll definitely stay two nights, and possibly a third." *No if it's all right with you. No if you have rooms available.*

"That's fine. The Blue room is available," she said. In fact, all but the aunts' rooms were available. Four in all. But the Blue was both the priciest and the best she could offer. "It's got a queen-sized bed and a private bath. There's a small sitting area—"

"Is there a desk?"

"A roll-top."

A slight shudder seemed to pass across his face. "Tell me you have Internet access."

"Not in the room. There's a hook-up in the library."

"All right."

This poor man was going to be so out of place here. She nibbled her lower lip, then fessed up, "You know, there's a Hilton only an hour's drive away. You might be more comfortable—"

"No." He interrupted a second time. "This will be fine. Thank you."

Her conscience was clear. She smiled at him. "Our breakfasts are better, anyway."

"What time is breakfast?" He had the most amazing eyes. In the few minutes he'd been in her foyer, they'd changed shades. Not pewter now, more of a Paul Newman blue.

Since he was her only guest, breakfast was pretty much whenever he wanted, though she decided to keep her lack of business to herself. "Seven to nine, but we can adjust with a day's notice."

"Seven's fine."

"I'll take your credit card imprint now, please."

She wasn't a bit surprised when he handed over a platinum card.

"Are you visiting family in town?" she asked.

"No. I've got business in the area."

"Really." She glanced up. She couldn't imagine what business he could possibly have. She knew every person and every business for miles and couldn't picture a single one of them being involved with a sharp-looking man from New York City.

He sent her a bland smile but offered no further information. Whatever his business, she'd know it all soon enough. Beaverton was like that.

"Will you need help with your luggage?"

He glanced at her like she was nuts, and only then did she notice the navy blue overnight bag in the corner. "Right this way, then," she said, picking out one of the ornate brass keys from the board behind her and stepping around the counter.

She led the way and he followed. As they entered the hallway, she heard the muffled voices from the parlor. It wasn't tough to guess what the subject was. "We're serving afternoon tea at the moment," she said. "You're welcome to join us."

He didn't answer so she guessed he wouldn't be swapping stories with the aunts over cucumber sandwiches. She breathed a quick sigh of relief. "We serve breakfast in the dining room," she said as they passed the big room she'd set up so prettily with antique and second-hand furniture finds. She'd collected small tables and chairs of different vintages, linen cloths, china and flatware that didn't match, and that was part of the charm.

She'd have to remember to freshen the flowers on all the tables. She'd also have a chance to freshen up her morning menu. Since Aunt Olive only ate brown toast with raspberry jam and coffee, and Aunt Lydia had a bowl of oatmeal and stewed prunes every morning of her life, there was little scope for the imagination. Tomorrow she'd put on a full breakfast—who cared if it was only for one man's enjoyment. Maybe he'd send all his Wall Street friends to Beaverton for their holidays. The thought made her smile as they got to the broad oak stairway and climbed.

For some reason, she felt suddenly self-conscious. Naturally, since he was behind her on the stairs, chances were that her customer was watching her back. Big deal. So why did she feel this hot, twitchy feeling as though her denim skirt was too tight?

She was glad when the endless stairway ended and she

could show him his room. She loved the Blue room. Its blue and white striped wallpaper looked fresh and yet fit with the late 1800s period when the Shady Lady had been built. The four-poster bed was original to the house, though the mattress was new. She wanted her guests to have the best night's sleep they could ever remember when they came to her. It was, after all, what her great, great grandmother had promised when she'd opened the brothel. Naturally, she'd had her own ways of ensuring her gentlemen guests slept well. Emmylou relied on top quality mattresses, Irish linen bedding, and her bucolic setting to do the job.

She ran a quick eye over everything, but there was no dust anywhere. The room looked as fresh as if the last guest had checked out this morning instead of three weeks ago.

The chintz duvet cover, in yellow with green-stemmed lilacs printed on it, was as fresh as springtime, the ceramic jug and basin gleamed on the old washstand; the roll-top desk, which had belonged to the great Dr. Emmet Beaver himself, had the rich patina of age, and the old Axminster on the floor held the grooves of a recent vacuuming.

Her guest didn't say anything, merely deposited his brief-case on the floor and placed his overnight bag on the easy chair she'd set by the window. Two other armchairs flanked the fireplace.

"The fireplace works," she told him. "It's gas-powered." She showed him where the switch was located.

"Fine," he said again, sounding extremely uninterested in the fireplace. She supposed he wasn't here to curl up in front of the fire with a good book, or enjoy the view of her garden. Right, he was here to work. The room might be a little frou-frou for him, but then if you were going to stay in a former brothel turned bed and breakfast, surely you had a hint what you were getting into.

"I'll leave you to get settled, then."

"Thanks. Oh, do you have a list of restaurants in town?"

She blinked at him.

"For dinner?"

"Right." Her mind raced. Where could she send him that wouldn't have him speeding back to New York before his first good night's sleep? A sleep, come to think of it, that he looked as though he could use.

A gleam of humor flashed across his face and she wanted to catch hold of it. How it transformed that cold, all business countenance into something warm and teasing. "People do eat here?"

"Yes, of course," she said. "I'm trying to remember who's open on Sunday nights. I'll check and let you know."

"Thanks."

"Well, here you are then," she said, and stepped closer to hand him his key. As she reached him, he held out his hand, palm up. A strong hand. Clean, callus-free and ringless. Once more she felt that curious prickling at the back of her neck like a premonition.

When she got downstairs, she popped her head into the parlor just long enough to say, "I'm going to make fresh tea." She could use a cup.

She'd just walked into the parlor with the fresh tea and a few more sandwiches, knowing the three white-haired ladies were dying to hear about the new guest, when the object of their curiosity walked in. Since she hadn't dreamed he'd want to sit around drinking tea with old ladies, she was surprised. Even more surprised when she saw that he was carrying an overweight and rather smug looking tortoiseshell cat.

"Does this cat belong to someone?" he asked in that crisp voice.

"Why, Mae West, wherever have you been?" Aunt Olive said. "We were napping together. When I came down here, she was still asleep."

"She seems to have woken," said their guest, though that wasn't entirely true. The cat purred lazily in his arms, its bright green eyes only half open. That cat knew darn well she wasn't allowed in the guest rooms. Maybe she was trying to fool them into thinking she'd been sleepwalking.

"I'm sorry," Emmylou said. "Mae West is curious." She was also man mad, hence her name. "I hope she didn't disturb you?"

"She was banging on my window and howling."

Emmylou held out her arms, but Mae West wasn't having any of it. She flopped to her back and turned so she could bury her head against that muscular chest. Emmylou wanted to laugh, but Joe Montcrief didn't look particularly amused. He was probably calculating his dry cleaning bill, since his cashmere was liberally covered with cat hair.

"I'm so sorry," she repeated, taking a firm hold of the cat who meowed in protest. As she scooped up the animal, her fingers dug into Joe's sweater, and she couldn't help but notice that he sported a nice hard belly. He smelled like something they didn't get a lot of at the Shady Lady. Like a young, virile man. For a second she envied the cat, then gave herself a mental shake and dumped Mae West on the floor. With a brrp, the feline stalked to the couch and leaped to Aunt Olive's lap.

Joe was brushing cat hair off his sweater and the thighs of his slacks. Lydia, watching him with interest, said, "You look like you're packing some heat. Can't you get it up?"

Aunt Olive, busy stroking Mae West, said, "Really, dear. Not in public."

And Betsy stared at their guest as though he'd disappear if she blinked.

"Tea!" Emmylou shrieked.

Joe raised his head and gazed at the assembled company. No doubt, they looked like something from a drawing room farce, but if he said just one rude or insulting thing to her darling aunts, he'd be out on his ear and that was that.

"Thanks," he said. "I'd like some tea."

"I could bring some to your room, if you're working."

"No. I'll have it here."

Well, she thought, as she poured him a cup in the best bone china with pink roses, at least he'd forgotten about the unfortunate incident with Mae West.

Lydia, sadly, wasn't nearly finished. "Well, young man," she said, sitting straighter and giving him a glimpse of what a fine pair of legs a woman could still reveal at seventy-five years old, "you were wise to come to us. Did the doctor send you?"

"Doctor?"

"It's all right. We've helped many men like yourself over the years. An older woman can offer so much more than a clueless young woman. In our day, men didn't need any of those newfangled drugs. They had us, right, Olive?"

"That's right. We were human Viagra. Too bad they couldn't bottle us back then."

"Sandwich, Aunt Lydia?" Emmylou asked desperately. But her aunt waved her away. "What is your sexual problem? I'd be happy to help."

In her day, along with Olive and Emmylou's grandmother, Patrice had been what Dr. Emmet Beaver termed intimate healers. Lydia, however, hadn't grasped the concept of retirement.

"Sexual problem?" Joe echoed, looking dumbfounded.

Helpless to think what else she could do, Emmylou passed him his tea and placed a proprietary hand on his shoulder. In a case of desperate times and desperate measures, she said, "It's all right, Aunt Lydia. Joe is my client."

As her supposed client looked up and caught her gaze, the trickle of awareness she'd felt built up to a waterfall.

Those silver, gray blue eyes were shot through with devilry. "Thank you, Emmylou," he said. "I think I'm going to need a lot of one-on-one work."

Oh, oh. She had a feeling there was trouble ahead.

We don't think you will want to miss
HELLO, GORGEOUS!,
MaryJanice Davidson's next novel from Brava.

Available in March 2005.

There were a few flaws in her plan, she thought, staring dreamily at what's-his-name's hands as he shifted gears. He had wonderful hands, big and blocky, and the knuckles were sprinkled with fine black hair. If she couldn't stare into his big dreamy blue eyes, she'd stare at his hands. Oh, and think about the flaws. Right. That, too.

Flaw number one: she wasn't the killer.

Flaw number two: she wasn't sure he was, but on the chance that he wasn't, the killer was still running around loose. Killing . . . what did he say? Members of the Wagner team? She knew about them, they were the team that had infected her. Wagner for Jamie Wagner, the Bionic Woman. Ha. Ha. Ha. Somebody at the O.S.F. was watching too many reruns.

Flaw number three: she had just agreed to be taken into what's-his-name's custody for an indefinite amount of time.

Flaw number four: she didn't know what's-his-name's name.

Flaw number five: she was letting her hormones do her thinking for her, which, while almost always resulting in short-term satisfaction, led to long-term poor results.

Flaw number six: The Boss.

"That reminds me," she said. "I need to make a phone call."

"Where's your cell phone?"

"Pal, you're probably looking at the one person in the state of Minnesota who doesn't have one."

"*Gregory Hamlin sent a green recruit into the field without a cell phone?*"

"Don't yell. I'm sitting right here."

"Unbelievable," what's-his-name muttered. "Truly. The mind reels. The mind is boggled."

"Pal." She snapped her fingers. "Are you with me? Stay focused, okay? I. Need. A. Phone."

"When we get into the jet, you can use mine."

"Okay." Jet? Oooh. Jet? "Jet?"

"Yes."

"Where are we going?"

"My home."

"Okey-dokey."

She supposed it was time she read that stupid file. She settled back in the luxurious leather seats of the whatever-it-was he was driving (she had never been a car babe) and closed her eyes. And read.

Dmitri Novatur snuck another glance at the odd blonde in the seat next to him, and nearly drove into a telephone pole. That's enough of that, he told himself. Pay attention. Yes, she's quite pretty, but that's also quite irrelevant.

He had calculated several results from his trip to the motel, but the probability of her willingly going with him was only eight point five two three percent. The probability that he would have had to kill her had been almost sixty percent. He was, frankly, amazed she'd gotten into his Lexus.

He would have to re-do all his calculations, because as it was, he was playing it by ear. And he *hated* playing it by ear. Too many variables made it impossible to predict outcome with any accuracy.

And now . . . she was asleep!

He quickly calculated the probability of the Wagner team killer agreeing to come with him and then falling asleep in his car. It was low . . . one point six seven percent.

It was all very strange, and she was possibly the strangest of all in what he knew to be a very odd and cutthroat business. For a field agent, she was remarkably . . . real.

Of course, they trained them to be charming, and pretty girls were often specifically recruited, but truly, she was like no other woman he had met. And the amazing thing was, it had nothing to do with the fact that she was the *other* cybernetically enhanced human being walking around on the planet.

No, it was just her. When she wasn't yelling, she was . . . well, yelling. But when she regained consciousness, she had been more angry than scared. In fact, he didn't believe she had been scared at all.

Most agents, upon waking in the presence of The Wolf, would have soiled themselves in terror. Or at least cringed a little. Not this one. Not this . . . Caitlyn.

And what could her sinister motive be, to willingly come with him? Was he on her hit list? It would make sense, of a twisted sort . . . she had certainly taken care of enough of the Wagner team.

That was perhaps the oddest thing of all. She didn't seem like a cold, detached assassin. She was more like . . . like someone you might run into at a coffee shop.

But perhaps that was part of her skill.